And The Chalice of Tribute

Tribute

M. R. Davenport

Published by Sapphire Arts, LLC
3795 Lochner Rd, SE
Albany, OR 97322
www.sapphireartsdesign.com

My King
The Chalice of Tribute

ISBN-13:
9781691239412

First Edition
10 9 8 7 6 5 4 3 2 1

Cover Art by Louise Evans

From the Author

"My King" is an allegory. An allegory, simply put, is using a story to teach a lesson. Much like a parable. Many allegorical passages in the Bible, however, are real life stories.

Because of the nature of this writing, the stories and adventures of Sir Miratus (Mare-a-tus) and Sir Caducus (Kad-a-cus) may well become confusing. That was ne'er my intention. This story is written in an "Old English" prose. It uses many words that have old origins and are, for the most part, out of use. But they are still considered a part of our language. Latin is used often and, unless within a title, will be in italics for clearer definition.

In a serious effort to avoid the reader becoming lost at any particular point (and upon the insistence of my editor), I have included a glossary at the end. I hope this alleviates any stress in reconciling the gist of the story.

There's an old saying, "What's in a name?" Well, honestly, there is a great deal in a name. As you travel with our knightly heroes, you will see many names and references that may be hard to read or understand. Most names of places and people (and creatures) will have a Latin basis. You will find the explanations of these in the glossary.

So, yes indeed, names are important. For instance, in the Bible, God is called God because there is little else with which to describe Him in English. He is God. But if you delve into a solid word study on His name, you will often find that it is not always translated as it should. At different times the original word for God is more specific.

It can be the same with us. In America we often prefer the name over the life blessing it may re-produce. And names can be a blessing or a curse. So you may find that when a new character is introduced, a quick reference to the glossary will give you insight into that person.

For ambience, have Celtic music playing whilest you read. Just a suggestion.

M.R. (Matt) Davenport

"'Tis a fair thing I have done for you. 'Tis a fairer thing *He* has done for you. In immensity. And grander still."

-Sir Caducus, Knight of the Albus Civitatus

Quia Rex Meus

Other Books by M. R. Davenport

Hutch
Blaqwatch: 30 Days of Summer
My King & The Chalice of Tribute
The Joseph Project

Shadows of the Everstone Series

Book I: Ketchwood
Book II: Of Giants & Monsters
Book III: The Dragon Soldiers (forthcoming)
Book IV: Return of the Madman (forthcoming)
Book V: The War of the Two Worlds (forthcoming)

www.authormrdavenport.com

For Adam, The Man Who Spoke Of My King

I sat there, still to listen and understand
A good word, from a good man

Words of faith and lessons true
'Twas upon the pronounced, those few

A moment that struck as a reminder doth chime
Gentle and sweet, one and each at a time

Were such words the point of it all?
As I live and ponder and grasp my recall

For the note that he conferred that blessed Sunday
I could not expound or begin to convey

Sure, I am, that it was of power and might
For God, in the least, maketh the day and the night

Yet in it all, I know the message he put to me
One of wonder and one of merciful decree

From which the story haileth and gives me to sing
A story beautiful of grace and the goodness of My King

Thank you sir, and bless you in immensity!
Matt

Chapter 1

The City of Ementior

'Twas an honor to be called to the palace. Even as a knight these past many years, to be called up to meet the king face to face. I was elated. In my service, I had ne'er the chance to talk to him. To yet even meet him. Some of my brothers in arms told of the experience, but ne'er I. And, therefore, I were unaware of what to reckon upon it.

The way there from my home was a while. Two days. My faithful steed, Longwise, carried me since before I took a sword in my hand. He again carried me that day as I said my farewells to those I fought for (what yet remained) and took out upon the road that would bear me to a new destiny. I hoped he would have a quest for me. 'Tis the criterion for the first time upon the realms duty. Service to the king was a life of greatness, but a quest would write my name in the annals of time. Providing I were to accomplish it.

I took provision to supply me the journey to the City of Ementior (where the king's palace is), the dispatch communiqué, and headed forth along the nearby paths. Wagons seldom traveled to our part of the kingdom, so we had more trails than roads. Eventually I found my way upon the Bona Voluntate, the highway that continued north toward Ementior. It was a good road, wide and easy. Still I was, as always, very careful.

Longwise had been much in the stables of late and was clearly anxious to stretch his legs. It proved impossible to keep him at a gait, so I allowed him to run.

The countryside around Patrice, my home village, was beautiful this time of year. The rolling hills covered with green grass that befits our land so well. Tall trees and a lofty blue sky.

The wind was somewhat biting; but the journey would be long, so I continued to run Longwise.

The first of my nights while in transit was spent beside a small brook just a mile from the village of Oppidville. The town was smaller than my own Patrice and offered no lodging nor other fare. It was yet a day's ride to the City of Ementior; so I was up early, well before daylight. I remained outside of the village to avoid distraction and having my travel slowed.

Although I had served his majesty these past three years as a knight, I had yet to meet him. Indeed, I had yet to see the city. Or even take the journey there. Oppidville was as close as I had come. Mine was a small lot in the kingdom, and I wished to increase it many-fold. There was nothing if not to be greater.

The country changed ever so slightly as I progressed. I found it to be odd that the closer I came to the king's city, the less majestic the land appeared to be. It was disheartening. The road forced me to travel through a number of small settlements. Many seemed less than what I expected them to be, living in the king's valley.

The people wore drab, poorly made, and unkempt clothing. Few beasts of burden and fewer children. The crops that were on the way looked even less proper. The time of year that I journeyed should have shown healthy and strong wheat, corn, and fruit. The land looked badly nourished and starving. It grew worse the farther on Longwise carried me.

After nearly another day of travel, the city proper came into view. On a hill raised up and steep, I exited the sickly trees that surrounded Bona Voluntate. The land cleared, and there it was below me. Enormous as the sea. And covered in a cloud of rutty, ugly smoke. It was blackened and old looking. Diminutive in color and dingy. My heart broke for the view which I took in was nothing like what I had long imagined it to be.

She was round about and enclosed by a mighty wall. There were many outlying villages that were bustling to some amount, but they were nothing like the fortress of the city. Roads led from all directions to the great wall and each had an entrance.

I imagined in my mind's eye the great distant lands those roads all led through. Including the one I was upon now. Back to Patrice, my home. And beyond.

Towering above all that were included within the wall, the great spires of the castle thrust up into the smudgy sky. It enticed me, and I was anxious to meet the king; so I spurred Longwise down the hill and charged the road, heading quickly to the opening that was most directly in my path. The thrill of the day's eventual outcome covering me like a nap sack and blinding out anything that didn't seem to fit the picture I had built within my own thoughts of what I would see this day. All other concerns now flushed with the image of my king in my head.

◆　◆　◆

The opening in the gargantuan wall that lay before me was wide enough for a dozen horses. And well needed. I followed a carriage into the city grounds as another was exiting. I wondered if all the openings were so large and how in the name of all that is that they defended them.

The land surrounding the wall was full of activities beyond the imagination. As though a circus were there. But far more than just a few trained and caged, ferocious animals. Much of the enterprise were next to or near what seemed perpetual structures. As well as tents of every shape and size. Hundreds of people ran this way and that. It was like nothing I had seen before.

The grounds were worn and, in some places, muddy from a fairly recent rain. There was little grass. And of such, brown and drab like the remains of the whole area.

I greeted quietly all I passed. A tip of my homemade cavalier to the ladies and a simple nod to the men. I saw none that appeared to be any sort of nobility. Or jovial, for that matter. I got a few extra looks as my tam was a light blue. In fact, I wore my best and much of it was colorful. Something I saw little of around the city.

Once inside the entrance, Longwise's shod hooves echoed a clop. It blended with the others that traveled about me. The cobblestone paving was a nice relief from the dirty, dusty routes we had spent the last two days upon. Indeed, the whole of life in Patrice.

Though the castle seemed to be at city center, I wound through many wide, industrious lanes, filled with people and bustling sales booths, to find my way to the king's residence. The smells were sometimes pleasant, but mostly bothersome. Every type of commodity and service was offered. From broken down carts and wagons, to meat, to the bordellos. It was prodigious to see.

Those who were employed to fetch the sales were often directly in my path. A thing dear Longwise did not appreciate. Nor I for that matter. Usually a little rearing got them to move on. I was intent to see the king. I carried the letter from him requesting my presence. I would not let anything distract me from that course until it was run.

Eventually, I found myself clear enough of the marketplace that I could pick up the gait safely without the fear of running a person down. The roadway and buildings curved slightly, and I found myself with a massive cross street. I took it to my left and marched directly to the castle grounds proper.

The citadel did indeed stand tall and magnificent. But, like the rest of the city, a little drab and dingy. "'Tis a working castle." I reasoned with myself. The grounds around it seemed at odds with what the place was to be. A king's home should stand out, alone, aloof. But it was what it was. "Indeed," I said aloud and spurred Longwise to the entrance.

"You, there! Halt!" Off to my left a soldier approached. "You cannot just wander your mongrel into the castle. What do you think this is?" He wore a full chainmail, head to toe. A simple white and black frock overlay it. And a shabby sword at his side. He was overdressed. A chainmail at the castle front?

"Many pardons, squire. I was unaware..."

"Call me squire again, outlander; and I shall pull you from your dog and learn you what it takes to guard the king's castle!" He was now angry. Or, he seemed as such. I felt it would not improve my circumstances to repay in kind. I acquiesced as best I could.

"In that case, a *thousand* pardons, my liege. I meant no disrespect, honestly I did not." Of course, that was not true. He insulted the finest horse in Patrice. Still, I needed to be about my business.

"What do you need?" He demanded.

I held up my dispatch from the king that I had already retrieved, expecting just such a question. "I am to meet with the king!" I said it loud enough that anyone in earshot could hear. It was a proud moment for me. I thought I should be treated at least a tad bit better. He took the scroll from my hand and unrolled it.

"Ha." He looked up at me. "'Tis your first time here, no doubt?" He posed it as a question.

"Yes. But it shan't be my last!" As though that would cause a gentleman to suddenly appear. It did not, of course.

"Stable the beast, then proceed." He pointed down the lane to the east. Opposite I'd come.

I resisted asking if he were the stable boy. That would have gotten me flogged, I fear. "How far be yet the stables?"

"Does not matter. There are a dozen. Pick as you desire." He said as he turned back to the entrance of the castle.

I walked Longwise down the cobbles to the first paddock we came to. A sign on the front gate said it was full. As did the next four. Finally I arrived at the first to have nary a sign and enquired at such as to them having room about. The man stood looking at me. He was shabby to the greatest degree. He seemed to have bathed in rather than mucking the stalls. "Do you see a sign saying otherwise?" Was this city full of the demented and cross? The only smiles I had cast upon were worn by those trying to sell me creation.

"You're a snip as the guard was, aren't you?" He smiled. I dismounted. "Please take care of him. Some grass. Or grain if you have it. Not much though. I suspect we shall be on our way quickly. The king has a post for us." I went about handing the reins to the man. "And a rubdown with hay or straw." He refused to move.

"Five pence for the remainder of the day. Uhhh, ten for the grain."

"What?" I interrupted. "I am a knight of the realm, you fool. How dare you demand of me!"

He ne'er quit his smile. "I understand. There be around 50 or 60 today." He spoke some sloppy enunciation I was helpless to grasp and handed the reins back. "You needn't be forced 'bout it." He pointed farther down the lane. "There are five more stables 'long here. 'Bit in other parts of the city." He smiled bigger. "We all charge the same."

It took less than five minutes to prove he was being truthful on the matters of cost. I returned. He now had the full sign out front. I went to the next. "Five pence for the remainder of the day." He said. I handed him the five and the reins.

"I should like him rubbed down. How much?" I enquired.

"Should be 15 fer jus the rub, but I'll take 15 fer both the rub and the stall." I handed him the rest of the pence and proceeded towards the castle. I did not expect to purchase lodging for the horse. There weren't a lot of ready cash in my pocket. As a knight I expected to be treated with honor and welcomed into the city. But I was clearly mistaken.

The guard at the palace entrance was different. His dress the same, his demeanor as well. I pulled the king's scrolled dispatch from my satchel and handed it to him. He allowed me to pass with a smile. At first I thought it was one that bid me a good day. Then I understood it to be of sarcastic humor. As though I was in derision. A jester.

I looked about myself in unfit gall and turned to go through the gigantic, boisterous gates. It was an enormous place. A variety of ante room entrances and hallways spread about. I turned about again and asked the guard, "Which direction should I point myself?"

He smiled. "Follow the line, your lordship."

I did my best to ignore his oblique mockery. "The line?" I queried him again.

"The line." He turned to watch others approaching from various directions. 'Twas a very busy street. He pointed over his shoulder with the thumb upon his right and offered no further elucidation. I had it not within me to further withstand his discourse, so I returned and walked forward to the gaping entrance.

Many and varied were those I passed. Few appeared to wear much more than a simple smock or tunic. And, mostly, drab. No one appeared to dress for the palace as I had expected.

Inside the castle, which was made from the same dull, slate-colored stone as the great, outer wall, I found bulwarks far off to my left and right with a singular door in each. To my front, the structure opened to a number of halls and a few more walls with doors. Five in all. The halls, that is. All of equal width and height. A rounded archway top. Between the center one and the next outer two, were doors. Two, one in each. Hanging here and there, almost haphazardly, were great tapestries. Their colors appeared to exist, but greatly faded. To the point they no longer had a significant image. Or meaning.

I looked down the halls. I saw no line. I searched the floors and the walls and walked to the first great hall on my left. It did not lead to anything in particular. And was completely uninhabited. Then back to the next one. It was identical. Then the center. No change. And so on.

Finally, the last one, to the far right side, was awash in noise and activities. I do not know how it was that I heard nothing afore I got there. The design of the ceilings baffled the sound, I suppose.

This hall was a wonder to behold. Massive as the others. None different in size or design. But very busy. At the far end a massive table existed. Six men sat there facing upon me. At the right side, in front of the man at that end of the table, a long line of men in a variety of clothing styles and colors stood. At least 30 to 40. As well a few scattered in front of the others, but nothing like the right side.

I continued searching for the line I was to follow. As I did so, a man bumped me as he passed by heading inward. He apologized, and I stopped him. "Could you apprise me of the whereabouts of the line we are to follow?" I asked.

He looked at me. "Are you a child?" He laughed out loud and pointed to the line of men waiting to be seen at the table. *The line of people,* I thought. *How foolish of me.* He continued on; and I followed, taking my place at the end of this line. I was not, apparently, the only one to meet the king this day. At least he did not call my folly to the attention of the others.

I spoke to none while I waited. If all were to see the king that day, he would likely have much on his plate. I knew that it was not every day that one is sent on a quest. But my letter only requested my *presence*, it was not a guarantee that I was to be about a quest.

It was an interminable amount of time that I stood there. My legs were immensely sore. Yet I complained not. Regardless, I was indeed in a most honorable position to have this summon.

Longwise and I had arrived to the palace in the early afternoon. Apparently, it was rather a process to continue from here. As each was seen, first by the individual at the far right of the table, they moved to another. Once there, they were tended to and dismissed. After a time, a number of others gathered behind me.

An hour into the wait, while I was still ten or more from the table, the man we were all in line to talk to stood to his feet. He leaned a little off to his right side to look down the line of men. "Stolidus?" He yelled out across the colossal hall. From behind us, we all heard the echo of running feet.

"Yes, m' lord?" The owner of the clamoring feet yelled back as he approached. He was dressed similar to the guard outside.

"Go and tell Praetus to refuse entrance the remainder of the day." He blurted out, pointing to the entrance of the castle.

"Yes, m' lord." He'd barely stopped when he turned to rush back to pass along the instructions.

From behind me, I overheard another in line. "'Tis the most anxious guard I have ever seen." To which several tittered.

We returned our attention upon the master at the head of our line. It would prove to be another hour before I was called to him.

He wore a cloak of mixed, drab colors. It seemed less his station. I would have expected him to be garishly robed. Even his velvet-encrusted tudor was out of place for a house of royalty. But it seemed to be what I was to come to expect in a city that appeared "dingy."

He paid me little mind and stuck his hand out to me while still in conversation with the last knight as he had been sent to the man on the far end of the massive table. I placed my scroll in his hand. He summarily un-rolled it and laid it before himself. "Your name?" He asked without looking up at me.

"Sir Miratus, of Patrice." I pronounced, proudly.

The man look upon me as if I were some kind of fool. "Patrice?" He chortled. A glance back at the scroll and he scribbled some nonsense upon the lower part. His signature, I derived. "Step off to the end." He said, suddenly pointing to his right. He rolled the scroll back up and handed it to me, yet smirking. Why I was handled so quickly and most of the others took time, I learned, they were upon return treks from a quest.

I had thought for a moment to thank him, but it seemed fruitless and, doubtless, would be un-obliged. The gentleman's disposition appeared to have been left at the great door which Praetus now disallowed entrance. Possibly the beginning of the ramp before encountering him altogether.

I arrived at the far end of the table and got into a much smaller line, with only two occupants in front of me. In moments I was again before another man in elaborate, yet garishly plain, garb. He took the scroll, as the last man had; and in the same fashion, signed an illegible name upon the base of the vellum. "Proceed to Lord Literamet's office for assignment." He initially instructed me in a plain, boorish voice with no actual directions. Apparently, the vacant face with which I responded alerted him to my *puer terra* lack in the realm. So he added a succinct point towards the rear of the hall. "Out the door, to your far right. Lord Literamet. Go."

I took the scroll and proceeded. A few cackles were emitted by the other, apparently more well-seasoned, knights as I followed the directions given me.

I departed the great hall and found, within the massive foyer that I had traversed earlier, the two doors to right and left did, indeed, have writing upon the top edge. With closer inspection, I found the one on the right to have Lord Literamet's name carved within it. Of which, was of a standard size. The wall extended so high, I thought it possible I could not see the end of it. And likely 25 cubits in each direction. No tapestries, no windows, no other doors, were within it. The door did, indeed, seem tiny by comparison.

It was wooden with heavy iron works that appeared to hold it in place. I knocked. None within responded. I knocked again. There was still no response. I knocked harder. Silence.

"Just enter, you knave!" A voice behind me spoke. I did not appreciate being called such for the simple pleasure of someone incapable of being even slightly polished. I spun on my right heel, my hand swinging to the hilt of my blade, and looked upon the purveyor of the insult. It was the man who had occupied the table. The first I had come to. He saw my actions before I saw that it was he. "A knave indeed." He said. "You shan't live long in your quest if you learn not to respond so quickly and without care." He seemed a much more formidable opponent now standing still. "Open the door and proceed forthwith, young man; or you shall find yourself going home with your bungled dreams smashed to bits." He looked away and continued his march from the confines of the great room and castle.

He was right, of course. But I was still the fool. My anger ceased only because I did indeed wish to be on with my quest. The mission set before me. That which would make me great among the annals of the kingdom. I acted as if it had not occurred and entered the office of Lord Literamet.

The room was not as I had expected it to be. A low ceiling with a multitude of pillars supporting such. I could nearly reach up and touch it. The room was quite large. Much longer than it was wide. And it seemed to be the full width of the outer wall. The room was garishly decorated. The greatest brightness I had encountered since arriving in the king's home. At that far end, a large piece of furniture sat. It was like a table, but somehow different. A man sat behind it. Lord Literamet, I presumed. Being distracted by the odd ceiling height, the décor, and the size of the room, I hadn't noticed one idle point: It was filled of others. Knights, I presumed. Much as myself. Waiting, no doubt, for a quest. That all-important task to send them out to achieve at the risk of their lives.

The gentleman which sat behind the large table saw my entry and gasped. "Really? Is there no end to you quest hunters?" He motioned me forward. It was quite a jaunt across the floor to his table.

"Lord Literamet?" I acknowledged as I came to a stop before him.

"Ha!" He scoffed. "No, knave." I really did not like that word. "The lord Literamet, hasn't time to deal with all you...you busy-bodied quest hunters. He has more important duties to fulfill."

He stuck his hand out to take the scroll, opened it, and began writing something upon it. He dipped his quill a number of times. Finally, he looked up at myself. "Your name?"

"Sir Miratus. Of Patrice." He dipped the quill again and wrote it down upon another piece of parchment.

"Sit down. I shall call you as soon as it is possible." He glanced about the room of at least a hundred others. "Which I doubt it shall be today."

I looked at the others. Many of which were watching me and the man at the table. "Will it be this week?" I asked, smiling.

"I do not have time for your ridiculous humor. Sit, squire...er, knight." He pointed to the chairs.

I looked for a full minute before finding a place that was not occupied. It was on a long, un-cushioned bench. There were already two of whom sat there. One at each end. I bowed, as a true knight would, in introduction. "Miratus." I presented my name.

The first of the two barely acknowledged myself. He looked at me then back to the rest of the room. It was no doubt that the position we all shared was uncomfortable and difficult. But to be so rude as to not even return a greeting was unacceptable.

"I am Amica." The knight spoke from the other end. He stood and returned my bow. "Of Proculas. To the east."

I shook his proffered hand. "From Patrice. To the south."

I sat between the two. Most of the men in the room spoke with someone, just to pass the in-ordinate time. Amica and I continued our conversation. He explained that this was his second quest. His first had consisted of fetching the "Fleece of Rectitude." "It was an impossible task. Though I fought bravely, I failed. But I learned much in the process."

We continued to discuss the finer points of our life within the realm and the desire to meet the king. Others mentioned that they had met him. But upon a greater inquiry, it proved perjures. Which vexed me that it came to them so facilely.

One by one, men were called to be given their pursual. They each took their new scroll and gleefully left the room. Another six men entered after I. It was a dilatory proceeding. At length, and near forty without a scroll, we were instructed to return the next morning. Of which, I was ill prepared. With the quest came a small stake to supply one in the travel. Without a quest yet, I would be sleeping, recurrently, upon the ground. I became resigned at the realization that I would be doing so, mostly as I am about the quest nevertheless.

Amica invited me to remain with him. He, at least, had a tent established upon the eastern lawn. Well, it was more of a muddy plot than a lawn. An ugly area I passed as I entered the city proper. I gave it no mind to speak of then; but now that I approached it, I found 'twas nothing as I had expected to find outside of the great City of Ementior. The king's own city.

We both gathered our mounts from the poshly stables and trekked out the city walls to the Magna Gramina. The tents were gathered in a great circle within a circle. Within another. And so on. Hundreds of tents. Most of them only the size a single knight would carry. His was deep within the pile. "It is well insulated." He looked at me as we weaved between the others. "Not the variance of chance a scoundrel or rogue would venture this far to steal. Nary a copper."

Momentarily, we found his tent. It lay within a pile of possessions on the muddy ground. "Cursed." He yelled, kicking the wet dirt, flinging it here and there.

"Is there some amiss?" I asked. Both honestly and comically. A great deal, indeed, seemed to be amiss.

"Yes." He conceded. "But mostly, the flagitious tore it down." He gritted his teeth and curled his fists. "Miscreants!" He gathered his belongings; and we worked to load what was left upon his horse, Feather.

"'Tis alright, my friend. We shall find something without the crowded mud hole." I encouraged.

"It was the crowded mud hole that made it safe to leave in place." He snickered silently. "Which, now I see, is not that safe to begin with."

We did, indeed, find a place outside the other circles to set up. The tent had been slightly damaged, but not enough to keep it from doing as it was intended. Amica and I shared what little we had for food and night fell around us.

As morning began, we closed the tent in a simple plication and loaded it upon Feather. We found our way into the inner stables and left our steeds in the care of the same lesser equerry. The guard wanted our letter to look upon. He had to check our names against a list that Lord Literamet's man had sent. Finally, we were allowed entrance into the castle. Whereby we found ourselves, being amongst the earlier risers, resting quietly in a more agreeable chair, once again, awaiting our quest.

In no more than an hour, my new friend and fellow knight, was called upon. He had explained that it was rude to enquire after one's quest. So, of course, I was left with not knowing dear Amica's destination. I did, still, encourage and prod him to be incontestable about his forthcoming charge. "You will succeed this time without a doubt." I shook his hand. "I shall find my way to Proculas someday and look for you, my friend."

"I do look forward to it." He smiled.

"Thank you for your conviviality and generosity." I said as he left my presence.

I resumed my chair and waited until mid-day before the man at the table called my name. I stood before him, scarcely before he completed saying it. "My good man, where is it that you are sending me?"

He looked up from what was quite an enormous pile of parchment and skin. He tried to smile. He was a very put away and sorrowful man. He pulled a sheet from the stack purely at random. He ne'er took his eyes from mine. It seemed to be some kind of act of rebellion. One, the likes of which, had little to no planning whatsoever. Without discerning what the quest was, he gave it to me. I looked at it. He pulled it from my hand. He looked at it, frowning, and then handed it back. He began writing something down. He stopped and looked back at me. "My deepest apologies." He muttered. "For the records." He handed over a scrawny leather satchel that contained my pecuniary abetment. The coins chinked of lack. Paltry by any measure, but none the more than I would need.

My heart and mind raced. I had my quest. But at the same time, I fought within myself to understand the whole process. How ridiculous it was to observe. At the rate with which he wrote, the assignments could be in place for each person in just a matter of an hour. Or less. He pointed to the door. "Be gone, you young rapscallion!"

The room about me erupted in laughter as I chambered my quest wherewithal. I even found myself giggling. I did indeed charge the door with thanks and was all the way to Longwise before I presumed to know where I was bound. I pulled my faithful from the stables and prepared him for the trip. Once he was ready, I took the skin, which I had rolled and stuffed within my haversack, and read it.

A small effigy had been scraped upon the pelt. It was some form of a goblet. But in a strange and hard to recognize form. "The Chalice of Tribute." I read aloud. "Your quest is to obtain it at all costs. If you fail, make certain it cannot be used."

I looked at Longwise. "'Tis a great deed we are set to, my old friend." I looked again at the old skin. The only direction that the quest gave us was to travel the south bound upon The Arbitrium Highway ending in what appeared to be an island. I mounted Longwise and spurred him forward. Patrice was to the south. "We will swing into home and proceed from there."

Multitudes, multitudes in the valley of decision!
For the day of the LORD *is* near in the valley of decision.
Joel 3:14

Chapter 2
The Arbitrium Highway

The way home was of little trouble. Nevertheless, I do recall much occasion that I ceased momentarily and turned about to look back upon the trail. It seemed beyond my understanding, but there, near the roadway, were many acres of crops that appeared old and destitute. As though starved of water and necessities. The farther along I traveled, the less common it became. Such was the fact that, as I drew a greater distance from Ementior, the crops, trees, bushes, and grass became healthier and greener. Indeed, even the weeds alongside the road mended and appeared greater in number. It was not readily apparent as the change was quite gradual. But having noticed it in my approach to the city, I observed the inverse with my departure. A strange and odd thing to which I could not ascribe a reasoning.

Longwise and I continued our march to the south. As I had on my way to the king's city, I spent one night at the river near Oppidville. Then, early on the next morn, by daylight, I was upon my way. My excitement as to the coming quest was such that I felt already accomplished. Already surmounted with expectations.

By mid-day I was back on my home lands. I could see the tower spiral from the ancient, abandoned church in the distance. Everything seemed right, and I felt merry to my innards. "For the glory of the kingdom, Longwise!" I shouted, pulling my sword and pointing it towards home. We left the trot and charged home as though victory was already my own.

As I entered Patrice proper, my sword already scabbarded, I trotted my steed through the one bare dirt street, glancing here and there, smiling at the folks as though they understood my presence to be more than just an average knight traipsing amongst them. Of course, I was but the only one who understood the glory of the moment. I continued on towards the homestead south-east of the stores and stables.

I dismounted from Longwise at the stones of my family. Our generations back as far as could be recalled, lay underneath the old homestead. I turned Longwise out to the pasture. "One night, my friend. Only one night and we be off for the south and the Chalice of Tribute."

Having been the only one of my family who lived (or at least remained alive and in place upon our family lands), I had no idea how to care for the animals and few buildings that were there while I was about the quest. Upon my leaving for the great city, I had given the task of propriety to the one person who was given to help with the place. He was Certus and had worked many years for our family. With the sheep and the horses. And the garden that fed us. He heard my approach and came to greet me.

My friend caught Longwise and gave him feed and a rub. A stout repast, some promises, and good banter later, I collapsed in my old bunk for an unyielding night of sleep. Yet, well before daylight, Longwise was ferrying me down the roadway to join the Arbitrium Highway. Knowing that my purse was near to empty (omitting the few coins that were presented inclusive of the quest), Certus had filled a terrycloth bag full of dried fruit, hard breads, and preserved meats. Enough to last me weeks if I were chary. Hunting would be fine when I needed to, but it often led to problems because hunting on the king's land carried a severe fine. And most the land about was his.

Certus roused well before myself and had all ready. I placed my hands upon his shoulders. "Old friend, you have served my family and myself well for years. 'Tis a dangerous quest I am upon." I looked off and smiled. Then back to his face.

"Oh, m'lord, dangerous?" He begged in humor.

"'Tis likely as not, still." He grinned to me as much. "Should me bones not return, the chattels and holdings be yours."

"Dear lord, I am grateful..." He bowed in mockery. "Do not be foolish, Miratus. You'll be back."

I laughed a bit more. "I do think as such, but who knows to the end?"

Some hours after daylight, I was still at a loss as to where the highway began. There were no signs and no clear suggestions of it. Eventually, I found myself stopped at a divaricate in the road. In fact, it went three ways. I feared if I chose wrong, it would take days from my quest. I spent less than a moment of thought before I determined upon a tracing of my way there back to a farm whereupon people worked the fields. One closest to the road I called upon. "Pardon, good sir. Could you possibly shepherd me towards the Arbitrium Highway?"

The old man had a large brimmed hat that kept his face from the sun. Truth was, at that moment, I did not know he was old. I merely based the assumption upon the fact that he was bent and moved slowly. I heard a snicker escape from under the straw brim. "Is there something humorous? Pray tell me that I may join in the jest." I said.

He rocked back onto his old legs and, finally, looked up at me. He was indeed old, but precipitately so. He smiled. Not a smirk of geniality. No, but more, may haps, of contempt. It might have even been a bit of evil about it. "Yesh...you seek the fale of decision. Yesh, you fill be sorry. 'Tis better to be ignorant, my fwiend." His flaggy southern accent and lispy speech made it nearly impossible to grasp his didactic mumbling.

"My pardons, old man. I have not the slightest understanding of your meanderings." I fought to hold Longwise in place. He seemed to want to be on the way more than usual, suddenly. "Can you not just speak, pray so, of which of the forks take me to the Arbitrium Highway?"

He looked off towards the fork in the road. "Deys no sign dere." He pointed. "Deys dono fants yous to goes dere. But deys dono block de roads." He frowned. "Nufin dere fors yous."

"Your wrangled speech is annoying. Can you not just speak straight?" I insisted. My equanimity nearing its terminus.

He bent his head back down and shook it. The old, leathery face disappeared. "Goes, fools boy. You fill learns the troof and ner'r returns." He breathed deeply. "Takes de middle fork."

I was able to finally disseminate the last part. I had no reason to believe him. Or not believe him. And, in all honesty, little time to decide one or t'other. I reared Longwise about and headed back to the fork.

The three directions were distinct. The one to my left turned fiercely, sharp and immediate, into the deep underbrush. So thick a fly could scarcely pass through it. It disappeared quickly as it meandered a crooked path.

The route to me sword hand did very little different except that it did so to the right. In moments, it was gone from sight as well. Both were narrow and rough. As though seldom traveled.

However, the path that was directly before me was not winding, nor difficult. It did not fit with the others. It lay straight before me. Wide and inviting. "I suspect I could have decided upon this way wholly upon my own merit and intelligence." I said to Longwise. A feeble prodding and, with the road being flat and capacious, he gaited out upon the highway, most willing and contented.

The way down the road was comfortable. The surrounding woods appeared manicured and airy. It was some time in the afternoon by then; and despite a strong sun over my shoulder, it was cool and comfortable. Longwise stretched out at a nice cantor, leaving a regular 3-beat rhythm by which to commune with the nature about he and myself. It gave way to a song. Which, in turn, gave way to a silvery echo through the trees. I had spent a confined time orally with others, but my voice seemed to be approved of by my companion. Of course, I was his drink and fare. He did, nonetheless, repeatedly twitch his folic ears.

The Arbitrium rose, graceful and gentle, to a point whereby I could gaze upon the land before us. The valley fell away, beautiful, colorful, and wide. In the distance, the light became hazy and the points of interest became hard to distinguish. I could see the highway continue below me, slowly turning here and there. It was indeed a very gentile route. I knew within me that my quest would increase in difficulty and danger. Yet at least the way there would be easy.

In the most immediate purview, I could see a hamlet of fair substance. The border to which divided us was an immense canyon that flowed within it an equal river. As I could best surmise, the Arbitrium crossed upon a long, narrow span of some sort and into town, proper. "A fitting place, it appears, for a knight to spend an evening." I patted Longwise's neck. "Comfortable enough for even the master of the hoof that you be, eh Longwise, my friend?" He scuffed about and rattled his head. "As you wish. Let us proceed." I reigned him in a bit and let him lead out down the hill and onward to the river canyon before us.

It was some time before the bridge came again into sight. But suddenly it was there. A long straight stretch brought it into view as the woods and undergrowth gave way to the edges of the canyon. The bridge was indeed long and narrow but only slightly less than the roadway itself. I resisted the urge to get Longwise up from his normal gait into a trot. I loved the sound of a trotting horse upon wooden planks. The likes of which this bridge was no doubt made.

As I came closer to the bridge, which was painted all red, I saw that a large gate was slowly swinging into place. Effectively blocking my passage. It was tall and formidable. And nothing Longwise on his greatest day could jump. To the right of the bridge stood a large, thick patch of brush. Ugly and out of place. From behind this out-crop stepped the largest man I had ever seen. Or, yet, creature would be a nearer word. He was every bit of 6 cubits or more tall and had equally broad protruding shoulders to match his height. He was unkempt and bitter to look upon. He carried a very large club in his right hand. His beard, black as night, was grossly over proportionate to his pockmarked face. His clothes were torn and fit him poorly. His skin was a very light shade of green, and he had slightly pointed ears. Much to my dismay, there beside the gate stood a Troll!

He grinned a defiant and humorless smile. A grunt of pleasure sounded from him. I was yet 30 cubits or more away and could hear the sound well. Looking back now, I am certain that distasteful odor was already present. It alone would have done well to bring an army of pages (may haps squires, even) choking with tears and paled faces, down upon their wobbly knees. As though the creature hadn't bathed in the span of the amount of years he'd been thrust onto the continent. Since birth, as likely.

I slowed Longwise to a stop and dismounted. At the very least, I could approach the beast prepared to bring him down to my own level. My sword remained in its scabbard, but I pulled it out ever so slightly to ensure it would not snag per chance I needed it hasty. As I was want to do, my travel garb consisted of simple coverings. I had left my cavalier at home and replaced it with a simple leather and metal helmet. Upon my constitution, I wore a plain, linen tunic my mother had made for my father many years ago. It was customary to have an un-marked tunic until one has accomplished one's first quest. So, despite being a duly representative of my king, I was induced to verbalize it rather than have it bared obvious upon my person. Under the tunic I had on my long-sleeved hauberk. Linen trousers and half-greaves upon my leggings. Longwise wore no barding. It was too costly. As was armor. I would have to rely upon my hauberk and greaves. And my trusted sword.

The monster breathed a bit of a snicker as I approached him. He was great in height as I came close enough to fully indulge his presence. I noticed a few flies that roamed about his person while he stood there. Indulge may be an improper word for what I encountered up close. "What is that awful redolence?" I asked, both to imply the insult as well as honest curiosity.

He responded to my insolence with the deepest and most irksome sounding voice. At least to that point in my woeful life. The noise (for it was nothing like a voice of that which any had heard upon the entire earth – nothing close to a sound of correspondence regulated betwixt anything normal) reverberated back and forth amongst the trees and hills. And I do not believe he was even yelling at that moment. Like the racket of the giants of legends and odes. "I am Fastus. You will defeat me if you plan a night upon the Rubropontem."

"I plan nothing, ogre. Only to continue the southward advance." I replied, forthwith.

He huffed at me. "Do not mock me, child. I have eaten the bones of men far greater than you." He advanced but a few cubits and stopped. He raised the club, which I now saw was a size more than myself, and pounded his opposing palm with it. "You have ne'er faced any like me. I can see the terrible lack of warfare within you. I shall therefore give you but a chance."

"I need no chance with you, monster. I shall cut you to my size and have my say with you." In the hallows of my thought, I knew I was severely out-matched. But I also knew showing weakness was not a policy that would prove myself better than the troll. I pressed my luck with him.

He laughed loudly. "You may travel to the east or the west." He nodded his thick, hairy noggin to his left and then right. "You may return the way you have approached. But you may not cross the narrow to Rubropontem." His voice carried as though he hadn't sipped a drop of moisture for days upon the sands of a desert. None of which were within our vicinity.

I looked upon the left and right and saw that there were, indeed, roads heading off in each direction. Merely trails and, I surmised, treacherous and difficult. "Yes, I see there are other routes, monster. But I wonder their merit. How far must I travel before I am able to cross the river and return to the Arbitrium Highway?"

"Haha..." He bellowed in an ugly, nightmarish sound. "There is no way back to this highway. You have only to decide upon another way, return, or face me."

Without either fanfare or proper decisionary purpose, I charged him, drawing my arming sword as I did.

'Twas upon a dark night I had the chance to come by that sword. It was the last object of my father's possessions. He handed it to me from the confines of his bed, moments prior to his journey from life. He had told me since a youth that swordplay would come to no good. I disagreed with him most vehemently. It was that posture that, I perceived years later, had stayed his desire to gift the sword to myself. As a young squire, I had come to understand many different swords. Yet none meant scads to me until that day. It was not anything inordinate or protracted, but it was mine and intrinsic to those who bore me and before. In mine hand, it had ne'er saw a drop of blood. *It shall today*, I thought upon it.

For the seconds before my haste, he was well aware of my intentions. The length of the wood bludgeon in his hands was, indeed, as long as I was tall. A simple four cubits. Simple within me, but most stately in a club. This gave him two perspicuously lee-ways upon my own: Reach and substance. Long before my blade approached his girth, the beast's truncheon connected upon my emblemless tunic and brought my forward momentum to an abrupt desistance. And an excellent carry-through drove me so much abaft

I found a desperate need to gain my balance before I was flat upon the rocky highway. I momentarily conceded the fall and then discovered my rearward thrust was even greater than I had thought. As I fell headlong, my lowers were flung in a perpendicular-manner; and I rolled feet first back and over. And again. And...once more. The impact of that mighty log the troll possessed was far beyond anything I had thus encountered.

The rolling left but a small soreness in me. My helmet had managed to retain its place and served to protect my belfry. But the mail had done little to foster my person. I fought to regain the wind that was essential to life. Fastus had failed to approach very close upon my arrival. I prayed he would continue to do the same as I was, for the time being, incapable of moving. My ears, nonetheless, worked quite well; and I could hear the behemoth laughing at me.

Longwise found his way to my side. I had forgotten, for the moment, he was there. I looked at him. The trusty, pale and cream-colored, devoted friend was somewhat different, contemplated from that angle. In fact, he was completely different. He was onyx black with a white-stained leather cinch strap mid-section of the horse. I appeared to have an audience.

"Are you yet breathing, my friend?" A man spoke as he dismounted the black.

It would have done me little good to be seen upon the ground as a page or a knave. Perhaps the knave callers weren't so far from the truth. I fought through the excruciating rigors of my malady and brought myself as quickly as I could withstand, scrambling upon my feet and upright. A momentary glance at the man who had spoken and I discerned him to be a knight of some form. He was dressed not unlike myself. Yet he did have an emblem upon his chest. And he seemed to be somewhat more well-prepared as far as what a knight should appear as during a quest. Or a challenge, as it may hap become. "Yes, I am well. Of course." I pointed at the troll still standing there next to the gate that blocked my way across the red bridge. "'Tis the folly of mine for approaching the doltish misfit unprepared."

The knight walked about his steed and bowed. "Yes, I saw the match as I approached. Indeed, he is more formidable than he appears." He stuck out a gauntlet-covered right hand. "My deepest apologies." He retrieved the hand and removed the gauntlet. He then returned the proffered hand, bare. "Caducus of Albus Civitatus."

I took his hand and shook it. I winced, hid such, and persevered. I was certain I had mis-shapened ribs within my chest and even the slightest movement seemed to be quarrelsome with it. "Miratus of Patrice, *et miles* Ementior." I made to look as best I was able that there was nothing amiss by equaling his bow. For the time, I was certain he was fooled.

He looked upon my opponent with, I hoped, eyes in fear. I dearly wished to not be the only one there who contemplated the monster's enormity and bulk. "It blocks the bridge." He stated the obliquely obvious. "Does he have a purpose for this duty?" Caducus looked at myself.

"The all that he has said is that I will not have a night on the city of Rubropontem tonight." I gestured towards the buildings upon the far bank of the river. "I presupposed he referred to the hamlet yonder."

The other knight looked at the city across the red bridge. "Yes. Well, I had no intention of spending a night wandering the streets there so much as I pursued a few more miles before dark."

"As did I." Taking an onerous breath and agreeing. "I am more inclined to be about my, um...business than a few ales and poorest tales." I returned. He scoffed a bit at the reference to the old rhyme. I needed to have a sit and looked about to find a series of logs strewn in such a way to appear as an ongoing camp. Consummate with a blackened compass for the fire. I meandered my way to the nearest and rested a moment. Caducus recognized the strains upon me and offered his water flasket. "My thanks, Caducus. But I have me own upon the horse." I pointed at Longwise and this fellow-knight retrieved it for me. I would sit for an hour until my chest resigned, and I felt better.

After most of that time had withered, Caducus approached Fastus and would have a word with him. "So, beast, you are Fastus?"

The green-skinned colossus grinned at him with yellow and darkened teeth. Despite the time I had spent even this distance from the creature, I remained brackish from the stench. "That I am. What is your business?"

"Well, my good oaf, I travel the same as my friend back here." He motioned at me with his gauntleted right hand. "We wish to cross the bridge and continue our journey."

The gate keeping us from our onward march suddenly began to open. "You may go on." The deep, ugly mouth spoke. Then the troll pointed at myself. "He must defeat me." I worked my way upon my feet and made to move at Longwise.

Caducus responded to the brute with what I cogitated foolishness. Though, to be honest, I was grateful. "No, you do not understand. We both wish to travel the bridge to, and through, the town. Through Rubropontem. We are not interested in remaining there for the night."

"'Tis a shame." Fastus replied to him. "It is a place of great wonder. Your rejection of her is a rejection of me. And of my offer to allow you on your way." The gate seemed to close without the beast touching it at'all.

"Just as well, Brutus, I shan't go on if my friend cannot likewise." He turned and came back to our airy chalet.

"That was beyond foolish. Are you an imbecile in knight's wear?" I said to him.

He smiled. Not in humor, but in knowing. "You and I are much alike, dear Miratus."

I slowly found my way back upon the log. After I had sat, I looked at the man. "I do not think so."

"No, my friend. Though I have known you a moment, I know the cast that you came from. You are solid inside and of great character." He sat opposite of me and continued his daft simper. "You, indeed, would have done the same as I."

I dare say, I probably would not have. I am certain I would be arriving upon the far side of the gap ere we arrived at this point in the conversation. Despite which, and though I appeared dissatisfied of Caducus' actions, I was very much felicitous within. My quest was to be achieved alone, yet how I attained the point of completion was within my own discretion. If this fellow were to assist me in gaining the bridge and passage here, how was I to stop the fool? It was then I decided that I could follow along on the merry straight that he begun. Of all, I was certain, a small bit of a profit would curry myself before much. I looked him up and down.

I may even call him to course and have a notch in my lance before it was done, I
so thought. And with which I fibbed my way into an ally. "Yes,
given the same station, I opine, I would, indeed, most probably,
decline the opportunity. It would be the most honorable repose." I
stood, effortful, and, just as toilsomely, bowed in gramercy. "Myself
and Longwise, indeed, do thank thee for the heart of your fray."

"Fray? My dearest fellow, it was no fray. I had not an ounce
of fight within me to decide my goal." He smiled. "It is as My King
would have me."

He did indeed mention his King. "Yes. And by the looks of
it, we truly serve different Kings." I cocked my head. "Or could it
be that we serve the same, but for different reasons and different
understandings?"

"Why do you say such a thing?" He riposted.

"Well, in good taste, of course. But do look at us." I
exposited. "I do have a remarkable horse, clearly, but the garb you
have is more than I am even comfortable with."

He looked down at his own clothing. He was cloaked in
superior covering and arrayed with greater weapons and tools than I
had hoped I could garner in 20 years of fortunate quests. He looked
at me. "Doth my attire bother you?" He stood to his feet fore a
word could cross my lips and pulled his tunic off. He tossed it my
way and followed it up with the gauntlets. In moments all he had on
save his boots and knickers lay at my feet. He was near bare.

For most unfathomable reasons I failed to stop him. He
stood before me. "Would you prefer I rode or walked? I will gladly
hand off my Gallant if it should make you feel better on yourself."
He bowed as I sat dumbfounded and speechless. "Forgive my

underhandedness, m' lord, but I shall be keeping my boots and breeches." He turned and looked at the troll. Which seemed to be thoroughly enjoying the pastime in our camp. "I do wonder if he'd change his mind now." He postulated.

"I'm certain he will." I replied, confusedly laughing. "After all, with you being naked, he has no choice but to allow you through."

He looked back down at me. I smiled. "Not for me, you dolt. For you." He said.

"What do you mean?" I queried.

"You. You feel you must be of something great to pass through." He pointed at the clothing and accouterments on the ground. "Pick them up. Put them on. May haps, you could pass."

"No. They are not mine." I said in sternest.

"Well, then. You are lost and hopeless, are you not?" He said. He sat down. "I gave up my ticket to assist you in getting your own. Now, you rebuff my first offer."

I pointed at the pile on the ground. "Why would you do such a thing? It is embarrassing. You cannot offer such to a man you barely know. You apperceive nothing true of me."

"You said that I must serve a different King because of how I dressed. Because of my own weapons." He leaned a bit to me. "I deduced you feared your appearance kept you from the bridge as I was offered passage and you denied." He sat back. "Do you now see the dilemma I was in?"

I looked forlornly at the pile before myself and wondered what manner of knight have I come to fraternize with. "Replace your cloak, et cetera. There is no need for further occurrence of your unders. Please." He rose without further exchange and did indeed re-robe himself. I was moved, but resolute. I did not need this man's help to overcome a simple troll. I needed only to mull it over more.

It was a rare occasion that a man (even a knight) would go to such lengths upon a first meeting. So willing to give of that upon his own back to a complete stranger. I was uncertain as to think of it as gracious or as foolery. My ribs began to lessen, and I rose to gather my wits. Apparently we were both bound to the camp for the night. Of which, we had not been the first. Gathering a few pieces of wood for the night's fire proved difficult. Caducus volunteered to go farther out. "There was a delicious spring back up the way. I should like to take my flasket and refill it there. I will return with an arm of wood for the fire." I nodded, and he left on foot.

"Your horse, my friend." I pointed out.

He paused a few dozen cubits along and waved. "I think I should like to walk. 'Tisn't far."

I sat. And rose again. There was, indeed, much to contemplate upon. I looked at the troll. He stood as a statue, yet seemed to know when I took to gazing upon him. He would turn his head and look at me.

A friend loves at all times,
And a brother is born for adversity
Proverbs 17:17

Chapter 3
Fastus

The evening air was light, and the sun sat the color of oak leaves turning in the time of the Fall. Yellows, golds, and luxurious reds. I watched upon the far city. A nice comfortable inn would be a pleasure for the aches that my person now endured. I fathomed that I needed a less conspicuous approach. I had rested long enough. With my contemporary confederate off seeking ichorous sustenance, I decided to make another attempt at the savage withstanding us from passage. I looked upon my faithful Longwise as I wrenched myself from the log. A lance would be an asset at this time, but I was without.

I took to my saddle and reared the animal to gallop back up the road from the bridge. Just a simple distance for a superior charge. And charge I did! I leaned low into the nap of Longwise and put him strongly into the wind. My aim was the monumental forehead of my opponent. It beckoned me as the sirens beckon to the sailor on the coastal escarpments and precipices. And just as fool hardy and treacherous.

My straight sword still in its scabbard, I impelled forward, ever expeditious, ever fastened upon my quarry. This epoch, however, he was even more aware of. My presence and my stratagem. Disregarding the barefaced certainties, I trudged forward determined to spoliate the ire of my apperception and inhibitor of my quest. I was beyond reckless, introspective that my determination and irrational action would over-come the swine. As though that madcap maneuver alone was all I required to bring this folly to his knees, wherewith I could remove the atrocious capitulum and claim the first victory upon my quest. Yet, I had no

gimmick nor tactic upon my arrival. And, much to my dismay, I
had momentarily done just that. I was upon him.

With no reasoning afore the traipse at the demon, I pulled
the pedigreed blade loose and dove in but a single measure from
Longwise into the fray before me. I endeavored to bring the sword
forward as my lunge formed. For just the briefest of seconds I was
proud of my action. The sword did manage to pull forward and lead
my peregrination. Aimed haphazardly at the animal's right ear, I
fought to correct it towards the chest, the source of all life, with
great effort. The vast forehead so preplanned at such a speed was
unattainable. All occurring within the span of seconds.

Somehow, within the aphoristic contest, I am certain, I saw
him laugh. All caution thrown aside, I was on the wing with no way
to surcrease my momentum. Anon he summarily pushed my trusty
sword off to the left – my left, Fastus' right – via the ligneous
cudgel he possessed as I continued in at an invariable furrow,
landing with unimaginable accuracy. That is, my own visage upon
his enormous, balled-up fist. I do not believe he so much as
actuated, forwards or backwards, the breadth of a princess' finest
hair.

I landed, this time, a lump of so much swine fodder, in a
pile at his malodorous dogs. Which I had've scurried from had I
been about mobility. He cachinnated at the results; and I was
forced, due to my own impotence, to ausculate the grisly cackle. It
continued for at least a minute. I rolled to my back, hoping I could
continue my effort to abscond from him before he felt it his duty to
complete me. I discerned the flow of me own cruor draining from
my face. From the aperture of my speak hole and snout as well. My
noggin felt every throe, prick, torment, and misery that could be so
profoundly endured remonstrative of death. I was indeed alive and

my lungs continued to fill. The green brute moved off, continuing his goings on.

Oblivious of those involved upon my sudden need to slay this foul thing, I had put my greatest ally in colossal danger. While I dove headlong as the foolish knave I was at the mitt of my foe, Longwise, obedient as none other, charged, as led by myself, straight for the chasm that separated us from our continued journey. He had barely slowed his full gait in time to save a spurt into the river below. And while he did cease that dash, he'd yet piloted a slide down the embankment just a short purview. One that he wast not to return upon his own dexterity.

As I rolled again to my side, his predicament became obvious. It so urged me that I left my own pain and concerns as they were and rose swiftly to my feet, limping, nonetheless, to the edge of the canyon, a mere five cubits off, to behold my faithful down the side upon a slight ledge. Realizing the posture I had placed him within, I looked about for some way in which I would be able to assist him in his escape. The troll himself was nowhere 'round. The way back up was entirely too arduous and sharp for him to gain upon himself.

I slid down the declivitous ground to Longwise. He was beside himself. I rubbed him and spoke gentle locutions to him. He did, indeed, restrain and simmer. As a knight, I had ne'er anticipated the need for a rope, but a braid I now needed. I glanced upon the long, treacherous fall behind us. He would no longer draw breath had he continued on.

From my stance, I looked to the red bridge. It lay a scant three or four cubits up the hill from us. From there, it was that I could climb upon her, beyond the gate, and be on my way. I looked back at Longwise. Faithful as he had been, I saw now that, had I the desire, I could, indeed, mount the bridge. But upon my own. Longwise would be left behind. The climb would ne'er be conducive to my four-legged companion. The one I had known longest.

It was at that moment of contemplation that a rope landed upon the hillside to my obverse. My ken followed the cord up to the top of the bank where I saw my misplaced companion standing. I was meagerly surprised to find that he had a rope to begin with. "Of course, you are so prepared." I scowled.

"Mind the beast. You can scathe me upon his discharge from the precarious side hill. 'Tis a long way down." He replied to my satirical opinion.

I nodded. The salubrity of Longwise was, after all, my general charge. I encompassed his neck with the rope and the noose Caducus had heretofore fixed in the end. Astute that Longwise would struggle in the climb, I vaulted upon the saddle and held close. My fellow knight took the prod and backed his Gallant with a wary and assiduous stride to tighten and then pull on the cordage. It took no small nudging to evoke my trusted steed into the uphill clamber. "Longwise!" I teetered my voice. "Step on, old man. This you can do!"

The span to the ground above was not more than a few cubits, but enough to pour the fear of pandemonium into my friend's heart. He fought the circumstances to hear my advance. The rope was fancy, but I believe a consummate conclusion could have been achieved without it. Of course, I say that upon having completed the impasse. I likely, simply, desist the idea of praise upon Caducus.

That I was upon my first quest, I refused balm and maintenance. To have another provide anything would indicate my lack. Having it pointed out to the province, the class, the race, all of humankind. Notwithstanding that he and the troll were but the only that might ever know. *Quod perficitur per triumphum petis*. A quest is triumphal that is completed. The methods are of little burden or charge. Still, upon me own back I would have preferred the credit. Good or bad.

As my steed and I cleared the fringe of the bank, I trotted Longwise back towards the camp. I deflected the eyes of Caducus. I deemed him to be apt enough to grasp my distress. He did. I heaved him the noose pulled from Longwise's neck. He caught it in stride and took to convolving it to return it into his satchel. I spoke nary a thanks.

The white animal that was my closest cohort, took to cropping the sententious grass in and around the encampment. There was little for him. My satchel held a diminutive amount of grain that Certus had put in place. I had the funds to purchase more but nowhere, save across the red bridge, to gain such. I fed Longwise what I had. I needed him. I daren't believe the coinage would purchase a replacement were I to sneak about the gate barring my path. I rubbed him. He seemed somewhat eremitic towards me. For which, I blamed him not. The dreadful ordeal he'd just fought to overcome was entirely my malfeasance. My determination to prevail over the green and unseemly thing created Longwise's predicament. I was to blame.

Without a glance in the direction of the other knight's locale, I approached the mighty, black Gallant. He seemed to acquiesce my presence as I reached for his nape. I placed my hand upon him, and he shuddered his back. "Thank you, old man. *Pulcher equus.* Thank you." He raised that sable crest, and I saw the face of Caducus looking at me.

"Forgive my presumptions, my friend. But for the sake of your precious Longwise...I could do..." He spoke.

"No. 'Tis I who fought against the whole." I turned and began to walk back towards the gate. "And a good thing you were hitherto." I spoke over my shoulder. I reached the place that I had battled with the beast. After several minutes of scouring the grounds, I looked up as Caducus approached. "The creature has absconded with my sword." My head hung, and I shook it. "'Twas the last possession of my beget. 'Tis all I have of him."

He placed his hand upon my shoulder. "I have another. It will be yours until we have defeated this monstrosity and regain the one that your father gave to you."

I neither accepted nor refused the offer. The gate was beyond our crossing upon the bridge. At least with our keep and jaunt. I pulled away and approached the gate. I had yet to corroborate the proof of the portcullis. It was as it seemed. Stout and thoroughly latched. Immovable.

It was in my own judgment that I was unsurpassable. I had oft been braced within my own village. Not once defeated. Albeit, no one within my village but myself had ever been much more than scuffle material. A true fighter I yet had to cross. Until Fastus. Still, as of yet, a fight had not occurred. My simple forays into his presence had simply been rebuffed. Quick and facile.

"And from her, my friend?" Caducus spoke at length.

I turned from the block of our egress and smiled. "Thank you." I spoke, returning to the care of Longwise back in the open villa. He was capital, and I sat down on the nearest log. Off to the side of the highway, I saw a pile of sticks. I rose and seized them, dropping them an arm's length from the dry coals and began to establish a fire. Caducus sat opposite on the log there and watched. He had fetched his second sword and held it in his hands.

My despondency shook. I fought the brevity of my first quest. My head told me to relinquish it all and go home. "'Tisn't much, but it will arm you until we humble that filth in the brush."

I looked at him. "Why are you here? What is the travel that carries you to this camp?" I asked, half in sarcasm.

He looked into the flames as they began to leap. "No more or less than your own self. I have a quest. Something I am tasked to perform. One I would not relent to the greatest of warriors."

"And, as I am, it is within yourself and not for me to know? Supposing I was to best you of it?" I said.

"Wouldst you explain yours unto myself? Wouldst you jeopardize yours with myself being versed of it?" He responded.

"Indeed. I would not." I looked at the blade within his hands. I reached for it, and he surrendered. It was nothing to show the king. Scarred and chipped. A single hand sword like my own. Mine being constructed with great care and detail. This one, simple and utilitarian. For knaves and squires. "I thank you, my friend. I hope to drive it deep in the belly of Fastus before this time tomorrow." I said, soberly, in sincere hopes the monster himself had heard my rant. In the quiet of the late afternoon, the sound did indeed carry; and I heard the laughter of said creature. He seemed not the least perturbed or distraught.

We each tended to our steeds and made to prepare the night on the bare ground to repose. It was still light as we effectuated our berths. With a fire blistering from my friend's supply, we took a short wander back up the highway on foot. The bulwark of the bridge had bristling ears, and I would discuss things he were not aware of.

Soon after our distance was keen, the good Caducus spoke, subtly. "And now what, my friend?"

I smiled. "'Tis quite the monster we face. And you. You have chosen to face him with me." I searched for the proper elocution. "For which I am grandly thwarted and disenchanted."

"I am afraid I do not see the apologia within your rationale. I haven't even a slight hint of hypocrisy in my exertions." He pressed.

"No. And, in all due course, that is likely the premise instigating my fervor. Your simple motivations are genuine." I finished, and we both fell into deep thought. It became only the noise of the forest around us and our stride for the next hundred paces.

At length, he paused in his walk and faced me. "Such a reserved and quiet road for one so called a highway." I nodded in agreement. We'd scarcely seen little but a few squirrels since we'd encountered the troll and each other. Lively as they were, we'd have one for food were it possible. "Well then, how shall we proceed?" He nodded his head back towards the bridge.

"Well, I have tried twice. 'Tis your turn." I replied.

He laughed. "I had not thought this to be such a contest, my friend." He resumed his walk, and I joined in. "Such a thing should have much more a prize than simply allowed to cross the ravine."

I agreed. "Then, what shall it be?"

"I believe you have strayed from the intentions of my articulation. I meant the idea of the contest to be moot." He looked up the road that rose before us and pointed to a small trail that I had overlooked in my own peregrination downward earlier in the day. "That is the way into my kingdom." He noted with a sudden amends in our exchange.

I nodded to it. "Thin and tight. It looks labyrinthine and troublesome."

"It is. But it leads to the most wonderful of cities." He smiled, somewhat lost to his musings.

I decided not to pursue more erudition of his Albus Civitatus and stay on point. "The contest?" I asked.

"Ahh, yes. That." He stopped. It was clear that he desired to deviate along that worrisome, narrow path. For just a fleeting moment, I suspected he of an ulterior determinant to have me up that way and thus have me over-come. Then I recalled his having the upper hand on at least two occasions already. Rationale fought to clear my fog-enshrouded mind. He stopped and turned about, looking back down anent the gate, now just barely perceptible through the over-hang and crowding of the trees and brush. "'Tis not a contest. There's a great beast that is to be over-come. For us, we both now have the need. Because I refused to travel without you, I am in collusion with you. Though I am still of the same mind as I was at the time I turned away from Fastus' offer of free passage, I could not change it now had I wanted. And I do not want to."

"Very well, good knight." I said, resignedly. "That mecca is ascertained. The beast must be put down."

He looked upon me as though I had driven a blade into him. He placed his right paw upon my left shoulder. "My fellow paladin, you are still not grasping the needs. We needn't put him down. We need only defeat him."

I saw no difference in what he postulated as separate ideas. I felt no need to argue them. But I asked for him to clarify.

"Defeat and death mayhaps be different things." He explained.

In the slightest of mocks, I returned. "My pacifistic companion, they may well be different. But the possibility that they are not should be weighed. Just to be trustworthy in the effort."

He considered this with a sterned look at me. "Agreed."

"Very well, then. How should I carry on?" I asked.

He laughed. "You blithe, dimwitted loon! All of this and you are still upon your own." I made to look as profanely confused as a first-day knave being called to a knight's work. "Do you really...?" He searched his apex for the words. His chagrin shamed him. "*Quaero unum elicui.*" The old motto seemed to burst from him.

"You shout that at me? 'Tis our lot. You and I. We face our quests alone." The vision of my earlier conclusion - *Quod perficitur per triumphum petis*, a quest is triumphal that is completed – whirled about in my head. I desperately antagonized the idea of returning, quest accomplished and in hand, knowing that I had needed a benefactor at any level. "*Ego potest hoc facere.*" I responded, just as loud. "We do not need each other." Which upon, the following silence near deafened myself. I inclined to return to the camp.

"And, the imperative? What of that? Shall you turn to the east or west in hopes, perchance there are other bridges?" He spoke after me.

"I shall over-come him." I stopped and looked back at him. "Thrice is the grace." I quoted him.

"*Fatuus vobis.* You fool. 'Tis "thrice the cat died." You will not sustain a third blow from Fastus. Not upon your own merit." He said with finality. "Not even on the greatest of the days of Longwise. Dare I say your own person."

The self-righteous knave had sunk to insults. His own sword tenanting my scabbard came quickly into my hand, and I drove at him. Our detachment was nare a few handbreadths. More than he required to respond and prepare. Yet, he refused. He remained still, and his shank remained untouched. To the point that I brought me own upon his head without an utterance of migration or flux. As his life lay within my swing, I veered as I could; and the blow did, indeed, impact his helmet. Deflected by my purposeful vary, it did him no harm. In myself, I was thankful he wore the scrap. Nonetheless, he was knocked to the ground; and his head cover flung off to the edge of the roadway. I looked upon him. "You knave. Defend yourself, fool!"

"Against who? My friend?" He said, looking up at me.

"I am not your friend." I returned to my walk back to the camp.

"*Plus unum sumus.* You cannot pass alone. You cannot defeat him alone." He spoke after me.

Without a return gape in the least, I spoke. "You are not upon my quest."

I could hear his rising from the ground. "For now, I am. We share the same needs. We must both cross."

I stopped. A lingering consideration impacted my cogitations. I turned. He was a weak-minded simpleton. I realized that it were possible to complete this first hiccup and be rid of him later. Nary a soul to discern the truth. Yet, to acquiesce too sharply might betray my intent. I looked back at the bridge. It was most likely true that another attempt upon the green custodian would be to my dismal end. Caducus made no move.

The code of the knight upon his quest also bounded through my wit, reminding dutifully that it was the quest, not the means which reigned upon the supremacy of importance. I glanced back and forth betwixt the gate yonder and the squire. "Very well." I caved. For the greatest of personal dialectics. "Pray tell me, what plan have you that will bring the thing to his knees?"

The contrivance of Caducus, as I have now come to call it, was not one of war. It was not the battle plan that would be of great remembrance or written of. He had, indeed, thought it through and thus explained it about me and with detail. Its own solidity was as faulty as I had heard. To that point or since. He was certain, still yet, the contemplation was imbecilic-proof. The idea was as such that I could only concur within a singular premise.

"So speak it. I shall do as you wish, *foedus meum.*" He agreed.

"At this conclusion, surmising its failure. We proceed as I see fit." I grinned a surreptitious grin.

Caducus raised his sword. "So be it." I crossed his weapon in agreement. He scabbarded his and nodded. "But it will not."

◆ ◆ ◆

Rather the night there on the ground, we gathered our goods, stamped the fire that was nearly out already, loaded our steeds, and proceeded to the gate. The Bain of our existence was already there. He'd taken notice of the charging of Longwise and Gallant. Readied, we led them upon Fastus.

He towered above us. His smell and demeanor assaulting us at every step. "So the knave and the fool have come to brace the master again. Have you neither one learned anything?" A menagerie of insults came to mind with such a dictum. But, deferring to Caducus, I fought to remain silent.

"Yes, Fastus. We have returned to you. You are the guardian of this gate, and your great wisdom is all that decides the fate of those who wish to travel farther south." He motioned towards myself. "My friend and I see that you are, indeed, the master here. We do wish to grant that fact upon you."

"Ha!" He responded. He looked at me. "And what does the fool say?" Fool? I was at the least the knave! The contrivance did not append myself in the role of an elocutionary.

A moment with a trifle aught to say, I stumbled. "Uhh...my dear Fastus. Will you forgive my poor machinations upon your person? I am a humbled man. My sword is at your disposal." I knelt on one knee and laid the worn and chipped blade of Caducus' at the monster's feet. "Can you forgive my fool heartedness?" I begged.

All which I prayed would fail to garner the results my fellow knight had promised. This humiliation deserved nothing less than significant blood spilling.

"Well, could this be as I see it or am I to believe it?" He roared a doubt. But within it I saw a glimmer of possibility. I had no idea if the sword I had laid down would penetrate him. But I planned in that direction.

"My lord?" Caducus spoke up. T'were fine to play the fool. Or the knave. But call the thing lord? It was too much.

He looked back sharply at Caducus. "I am no lord." His anger crested a moment. I, for one, did not counter his assessment of himself.

"Forgive my friend. He only meant respect by it." I found myself speaking up. The intensity passed.

He glanced only a second my way then back at the face of Caducus. "You are good inside, so you and the fool may pass. But I charge you. This one, your friend, has much to learn. Remain with him lest he come to a poor end." He looked at me. "You have not fooled me. But for the sake of your learning this lesson, I leave to you according to the actions of your friend." He pointed at Caducus. "Likely the only one that you have."

All that was within me rose up. As though I fought the heart of my own self, I drug the reins of my faculty under control. The battle raged back and forth. I could hear the gate creaking as it opened just off from us. I locked eyes with the beast that towered above me. I could hear the voice of Caducus graciously encouraging me to follow him. I felt my legs frozen to the ground there. The honor within me refused to walk away. From that place came another wave of assurety in my own abilities. False as they were. The beast continued to stand there, his eyes beginning to glimmer with lambency. I believe he was beginning to become angry with me. Inside the argument festering within me, a voice of reason began a slow surgence. It reminded me of the strength the beast possessed. That he truly could fragment me at his own will.

The time I had now spent contemplating my attack was scarcely seconds. I have little dubiousness, still, that I was shortly in danger to face the last moment of my own fortitude. Had it not been for what I now know to be a much smarter creature than myself, Longwise of all that stood there at that moment, plowed into me with a definitive purposeful nudge. A "time to depart" look about to him.

I rose from my knee, took his reins, and followed Caducus onto the bridge. The wooden structure taking our weight with creeking and swaying. I forced it upon myself to not look back. I imagined I would see nothing. Yet halfway across the span, we heard from behind us the gritty, deep voice of the beast. "I take nothing from those who pass..." It echoed along the river below, up against the far bank and back numerous times. We looked at each other and then back at Fastus. As we did, we saw, from the sky, two swords drop and stick into the wood just a few cubits behind us. For a moment, I shivered at the idea a sword could have skewered myself. Or one of those nearby. Then I realized, he knew exactly what he was doing.

We gathered our arms and returned them, mine to me own scabbard, he to his pack. We continued on. I looked at Caducus. "How, my friend. How did you know?"

He smiled. "I asked My King for help. He has great wisdom."

"And how did you do that? Is your kingdom so close?" I said, half believing him.

"Yes, in a way. My King is always with me." He answered.

"What did he tell you?" I enquired. After all, his stratagem did, indeed, succeed.

"His name. Fastus."

I shook my head, not realizing what he meant. "It is the old tongue, I know." I thought a moment. "Jewel? Value?"

He stopped. "The word has many meanings." He breathed deep. We stood just as the bridge ended and barely upon the dirt of the highway south. "Quite often the old folks used it to mean pride."

I looked back at the great bush that was the monster's abode. "I didn't have to overcome a troll. I had to overcome pride." I said aloud.

"Yes, my brother. Pride."

Pride goes before destruction,
And a haughty spirit before a fall.
Proverbs 16:18

Chapter 4
The City of Rubropontem

T'was a scant dozen cubits to the first building of the city. Another few to the next, opposite, and the village layout in both directions there from. I had not the sense from the foregoing that the town before us was entirely red. Every building, some stone, some wood, some brick. Even those with which were clearly someone's home. Manor or shanty. All painted a red. Dank or bright. "What do you suppose was behind the idea of such a sight?" I asserted to my companion. He spoke nary a scratch. He remained silent as the dead windless evening that it was. Yet afoot, I stopped, Longwise's reins in my hand. I looked upon the man. "Caducus? What troubles you so?" T'was not a moment of compassion that rested on myself, but of curiosity. He seemed suddenly unwell.

He paused to look upon me. "I should not like to remain the night. It is best that we continue on."

I laughed jovially. "You jest. I have had a long and galling day. I seek, the very least, a bed that is not upon the ground." I pointed at a far building. "There, they will have a nice cold mead to sip on."

"Very well." He moved, yet reservations bewitched him. "I do not like the furl of mead, but I shall join you. Then we will part. I will gladly wait upon the south for you on the morrow." He insisted, pointing to the southeast where the far edge of town appeared to be.

I began my forward perambulation, nodding my approval but still at odds with my companion's notion. He ensued as well. "You are shaken over this?" I pointedly said. "You took on myself and the beast of the garrison back there. Now you rumble at the intimation of a simple brew? You indeed have me brain confused."

We continued on towards the plainly marked tavern. The sign upon the false front called the place the "Red House." *Unde oportet*, I thought. *Of course*. It was a slack and bedraggled representation. Indicative of a cheaper concern. Perfect for myself. I hadn't the slightest of Caducus' wherewithal, but mine was limited to the frail bag of coins.

Rubropontem was a bustling and hectic hamlet, awash with the plebian, the common, and a share of affluent. We were not the only knights in town. And everywhere we looked, there be red.

"I shall find a keep for the horses." Caducus ventured.

I handed Longwise's reins off to him, pulling my satchel down. "I shall meet you in the..." I grinned at the ridiculousness of the town's leitmotif. "The Red House."

"Aye." He replied. His worrisome ideas of the place were beleaguering to myself. I determined to not allow the *timoribus* of him to disconcert myself from a simpatico rest. Though my first day upon the quest, it had been replete with difficult, tormenting exertions and enterprise. I was obstinate about a pleasurable evening. Such would beg a good commencement of the morrow.

Expectations being as they were, a red-colored interior to the tavern was only natural. Yet it was as any other drinkhouse. The décor was commonplace and meant nothing. But my caution was not entirely tossed out as the wash water. I pulled the small, as of yet un-opened, leather pouch of coin. Retrieving the smallest of the lot, and I sat it upon what seemed to pass for a bar top. A five pence. The publican found his way to me a moment later. He was red haired (*quippe*), with a patchwork slop hat, and a quintessential apron that barkeeps have worn since the beginning of it all. Hairy as a great bear. The red fell upon him like rain upon the roof. I'd imagined the oaf eating a gooseberry cake and keeping the lion share upon his mustache and mutton chops. They were greater upon the man's face than upon most gifted promontories. I pointed at the coin. "My good man, what will that get me?"

Without so much as a grunt, he hefted the tiny marker. "Aye, caballero, that'll get ya good and drunk." He held it, awaiting my decision.

"Very well, let's do that. Sounds of an auspicious conviction." I smiled. "What have ya that be cold?" I roared.

"Well, me benefactor, that would be nothing. But the tap was cold an hour gone when we hefted it up from the vault. 'Tis close." He grinned an errant, near toothless grin.

"Then by the hairs of your mutty cheeks, that will do. Bring on a great one." I enjoined.

It was nigh on an hour before my companion strolled in. With him forbearing to drink the mead or the kind that might be a wee bit stronger, he chose a table in among the scattered patrons. Near the hind wall. A young lass took his needs and wandered to Barce, the keep, to pass them along. I sauntered, rather slapdash as I was toasting the mead by then, over to his table and sat down. I held my newest mug up in the way of the toast. "To the undoing of Fastus." I said.

He put his hand to his mouth. "Shhh..." He pointed to those around us. "They revere him. His defeat is not looked upon as a sterling accomplishment."

I grew quiet. I was soshed, but not beyond perceiving the rankness of the gravity of what the man modulated. "No. Are you sanguine?" I begged, quietly.

He appeared to feud with himself. I realized he was irresolute on if I believed him. "Come on, my man, speak up."

He relented the battle and gave it up. "I talked with a number of local bourgeois. He is considered some genus protector. Even though we did no harm and passed at his own urge, we would, at best, be run from the proper."

I sat still, leaned in to hear his whisper. "Me cohort! At worst?"

"They have performed hangings in the past." I pointed out. I sipped the sweet mead with my eyes wide and bewilderment.

We agreed to not mention Fastus or our encounter with him.

The young lass returned to our table with a glass of wine for my friend. "Wine? Why would you bother? It cannot be of great sting or even piquancy."

After the maiden moved along, he spoke back. Of all that I had seen him in the past hours, verm and of confidence, he seemed now quite circumspect and, even, introvertish. "There is nothing upon the menu I desired. I asked upon it for the simple need to have a reason for my lounge."

He did, indeed, sip the wine. It was beyond my capacities to countervail a fortuity to goad even the man who enlightened my venture across the red bridge. "Doth I see a boy quaffing a matron's drink?" I laughed. The mead had fully walloped my inclinations and stature. All portions of civility were set aside as I began a fierce attack on the man who'd been only good to me. It was that realization that plummeted upon my sorry functions at dawn. But well before I found a room and a cot, I found something about my friend that was troublesome and assuaging both.

Caducus sat stoic. My ramblings and taunts barely affected him. I wondered the course. With my head full of a pasty ground fog, I watched him after failing to goad him into a response. His eyes were fixed. I finally saw what upon.

The fair maiden who had visited our table much too often now sat across the room. She was comely and winsome. She was, indeed, much to see. And see, my friend had done in detail. "Go on, Caducus, old man. She clearly wants you as you want her."

What my ridicule had failed at, the words of encouragement did. He looked at me as though I had struck the damsel, rather. "What are you about? You spur into that? Do you not see how that..." He stopped. His great desire to remain inscrutable cracking. He had held himself upon the far side of the river, but now he began to splinter.

"Are you of two minds?" I demanded. "What strange tumult bewitches you?"

He bowed his head. "'Tis time to leave. I shall meet you upon the south."

As he made to rise, presumably to forsake myself and the Red House, the young maiden arrived. She spoke gently and sweetly. "Pardon, good sirs. Are you in need of anything?" She did indeed, evince my friend's attention. He reclaimed his chair, nearly charging it from its upright. I fought myself to not guffaw in such a cacophonous wail. It was, indeed, all I had. Caducus' stumble made his beguine of such pronounced conspicuousness that the whole of the room could see it. Yet, for the happenstance that it was nearly deserted, he'd have been made the colossal fool he appeared. Not that he would have taken note, with that damsel in his face. She was a beauty. She leaned in to his countenance. "My name is Disisderas." She whispered as such it was near inaudible for myself who sat within arms ken to Caducus.

"My pleasure, dear Disisderas...ummm." A smile that besieged the whole of his head appeared. He was so completely smitten forthwith that the presence of mortality about him virtually ceased.

"May I sit down, sir?" She asked with a voice like the sirens.

"Please, my lady. Do so." He positively sparkled with the charm of all he had within his knotty, sagittal head. A quick shift, smooth as the spines upon a dragon's backside, he stood and pulled the nearest chair loose from the table for her ensconce. I looked upon the deuce with indubitable deduction of the plight thereupon, I stood and pardoned myself. Neither of which noticed. They seemed to be one in thought and cared less for the atmosphere about them. I made my advance upon the bar to fetch another mead.

Of which I found myself moiety down, moments later, and pulled loose from said libation when a scuffle broke breech of me. I spun upon me stool in sudden scandal as my amorous fellow-knight flew at the door as if scalded by the witch's own cauldron. Expecting an emulous rival to stand at the table, rapier in hand, I beheld only the budding lass. Her face secreted in surprise. None about that could possibly be of shameful or dishonorable vivacity.

She peered at me with her arms raised in confusion. In frank disgust, I turned back to my brew.

In a trice, she was upon my periphery. "My pardons upon your mate." She grinned. I gazed upon her, now contiguous to me, her hand resting upon my right tributary. "He was...courtly." Her smile up at myself from this propinquity told me her age was not as I had presumed. *She is usus est*, I thought. It made me melancholy. Of which I could not understand. It was plainly manifested that her intentions were to have myself now that Caducus had decamped her clutches. My loyalties were upon myself and my quest. Then on those who would greatest benefit that. This harlot only desired the change in my pocket. As such, I was assentable to her alimentation. But I felt no inclination to her. I shuffled her off and left the House in search of a more notable inn to rest my weariness off. I feared that my response was already in homage to the man with whom I traveled.

What? A night with a whore? It should not have been anything less than such. But I could not. And that singular grappling propped my head vigilant and heedful the long night. The maiden earmarked to put me room orderly upon the day, most doubtless, disagreed with which she would be faced as I agonized and wallowed the night through. Alas, I did rest. Only to wake with an elephantine ache within my crown.

I found me Longwise. Where with had taken a search of near all the stables. Caducus had fled with not a word on his location. Of which he had paid the five pence for the night, a rub, grain, and water. I was grateful and thus found it triflingly whimsical that my steed felt a grand bit better than myself. I mounted the trusted beast and pointed him upon the southern route. "'Tis a thought, old friend. One which I trust only to thee." I patted his neck. "Perhaps the simpleton were correct. We should have continued and slept upon the barren, albeit safe, ground alongside the highway."

◆ ◆ ◆

The way south was a bit along. The red city extended onward. What lie behind the ruby colour and its obligation to obscure the entirety of the city was ne'er elucidated upon. I happily abandoned the conurbation deprived of that brief wisdom. I felt none less without upon my adieu than upon my ingress.

The Arbitrium Highway remained wide and easy to ramble. It began a slow eminence a scant mile or less from the last crimson edifice. I concerned myself with the whereabouts of Caducus. He who I had been better without. Thus was my speculation as my innards and my encephalon quibbled.

The gradient that was the underpinning of the highway's means and meandering continued to ascend. Long before I was mindful of the summit, I watched a meager trail of smoke grow from the ground into the blue of the sky. With close ascertainment, I could see the shape of a charger that stood adjacent to the road. It was Gallant.

Blame is upon feeble Longwise for the slight increment of gait. One could not guilt him for desirous needs of a good companion. He and Gallant had spent some hours together and had, noticeably, empathized with one another. Despite myself, I was glad to be in company with an ally. I was well versed in defending myself, yet *duo fortissimi* we forbear the entanglements along the Arbitrium better.

From behind the black stepped the would-be lover of distinction. I refused to admire him. Outwardly, *quidem*. He raised his hand in *saluto*. "Ho, yon traveler." He mocked. "'Twas a raucous night. The fairer of us, no doubt, withstood the temptations." He lowered his hand. With doubt on his face, he went on. "'Tis uncertain as to who that was." He bowed at myself. "My deepest benediction to you, my friend, for your decision to come cortege with a one the likes of myself. You are an honorable man."

I realized he did not mock. "I must postulate, you're the fool. A better man, I am not." I dismounted Longwise and nothing more was said of the night before. At least not within that moment.

The tendrils of smoke I had surveyed upon the climb came, as I suspected, from a fire my friend had built. Upon it a small pabulum was prepared. Caducus served up what was once hare. Whereupon he'd managed to ascertain this wild beast was ne'er explicated. Yet, the locale of its great demise was infinitely distinct. Me breadbasket lay empty; and the loathing that had come upon it with my noggin twinges had passed, so I was ready for even the most sparse fodder. Wee were I in the apprehension of poor Caducus' savvy in the quarter of palatableness. I fought, because of me own hunger, to coerce the meat within the confines of me stomach. I could not. Spat upon the ground, I looked upon him to see his blatant simper. "Dost thou dare to poison me to me own face?" I yelled. "'Tis as a bitter leaf dipped in the floorings of a donkey stall and fried in the guts of a troll!"

He no longer grinned. He began a caterwaul of laughter that echoed the canyons a hundred furlongs away. I could not resist but joined him in the vociferous and deafening clamor. It made all that had passed sufferable.

The sun had moved a good quarter before I spoke of the stumbles in Rubropotem. "'Twas an odd thing." I looked at the man. "I soon found her to be...less of the comely maid she appeared. I let her be."

"Ha. How genteel of you." He retorted.

"You need not expound. Still, so that you are aware, I am more than curious. 'Twas a sight seeing you dash from the place in such a manner." I rejoined.

He spoke, ne'er shifting his eyes from before us. "Will thou grasp a simple discernment? If you must ridicule, so be it. But I doubt your sense before I begin."

"I shall listen, silently." I assured him.

He remained stoic for several more moments. Then, "I dishonored My King upon my lust for a lady not my own. For a moment, I fought well. I rose to leave before my folly, but failed. Eventually, I felt the shame of the temptation. Of which gave way unto salacity. It was enough to drive me from the house."

"Might I say, you have recovered well." I broke my vow of silence.

He laughed. A small, mirthy laugh. "My King is ne'er angry. He is always quick for resolve."

"You speak of Him again as though He is among us." I replied to him, trying not to point to how foolish he sounded.

He looked to me from the saddle there upon Gallant. "But He is, my friend. He is."

But each one is tempted when he is drawn away
by his own desires and enticed.
Then, when desire has conceived, it gives birth to sin;
and sin, when it is full-grown, brings forth death.
James 1:14-15

Chapter 5
The Bravio

Difficult was my time of grasping this man's vision of his King. The honor he bestowed upon the Crown he so faithfully claimed. How was it that a man so gifted in comprehension that he would swiftly undo the mind of Fastus, yet falter in such avowal to an imaginary King. Perchance that this great Monarch were genuine. The Albus Civitatus a corporeal and intrinsic place. Filled with the clean and righteous that its name proclaims. Yet this conscript claimed Him to be ever present. It was upon the sudden distinction that I no doubt needed him upon my path. To which I would ne'er brandish such erudition within his ubiety. For as long as it were hopeful and expedient, I would remain in silence of such. As long as I could administrate our passage as one. In this understanding, it was apparent that my struggle of the man's obsession should remain reticent and taciturn.

The dialogue permutated from one theorem to the next. We talked of the sun and its paramountedness of the sky. How the mountains rose around us like the great walls of a monumental castle. We passed a few travelers. Caducus and myself giving way as proper knights should.

Post the sound of hooves alone for a hundred cubits or more, I presented a query that had been within my faculty for much of the foregoing. "Happenstance, my dear Caducus, were we to cross swords?"

Remaining his eyes upon the horizon yonder, he spoke without thought. "It shan't happen. We are confederate."

"Yet, supposin' our kings are at odds. What thence?" I persisted.

He reined in Gallant and looked at me from under his helmet. Longwise ceased upon his own. "There is not a fly speck of such coming to be. I would refuse."

"But this Great, Perfect King you do charge on about? How would He esteem your disobedience?" I prodded.

"'Tis nothing to concern yourself." He mused and dug his beast on forward. "It is not within His capacity."

He spoke with such finality; I nearly felt convinced of t'all. But I actualized that I was not. "Yet all kingdoms must reach upon new ground to pullulate and enlarge. Ours appear to be adjacent."

We rode on. He chose not to address my last posting. I thought it be a good matter to reprise another time.

The day began to be weary, and the sun we enjoyed grew lower. It was time to search out a proper place to retire. A fit and well-used station was found just off the highway a few cubits. Presently a fire was prepared, our steeds espied a robust patch of verdure to ruminate, and I set about trapping a young rodent for our own refection. Of which seemed readily procurable. Well enforced memories of what Caducus had passed off for victual the morning before made my hunt that much more vital.

When I returned to our camp, the fire burned well; and he'd prepared a spit. I stripped the hare and mounted it upon the heat. "'Tis a sweeping extent finer than me own." Caducus said after tasting the meat. I remained quiet. A good man knows his best. Whether it be with a sword or with cooking.

A brief time later, wiping the remnants of the fare from my face, I had agitated within myself long enough. Despite me best to keep it upon me own, I wished to know how it was that my fellow, of whom seemed all equitable, could be as such to reckon the presence of his King at any given moment. It just seemed without a sense of sagacity. Foolishness. Having none the ground with which to commence, I guilelessly asked, "Impart upon me the singularities of this King you often assert."

Awaiting his defence on the matter, he, instead, smiled as broadly as I e'er saw a man smile. As the grin that near spilt his head in the Red House over the lady there, yet even more so. Indeed, such that it even made myself some giddy just perceiving it upon him. "Oh, dear friend. There is much to answer that query."

Fearful now that I should spend an evening sleepless while he regaled this fanciful creation, I put my hand up. "Desist, please. I do wish to learn of this Incomprehensibility, but not His life epic. Retrench it for my sake?" I asked.

His smile diminished not a bit. "As you wish."

"Thank thee, my brother. Please, proceed." I encouraged.

The smile gave way to musings, and he began. "'Tis not a story common. At least, not as it was when it commenced. He was always. Yet, He had a rise." He stopped and contemplated me. "He is not a common king. He is not upon you to fight His wars. You do not increase in His Kingdom by virtue of your attainment and executions. 'Tis a kingdom zealous for peace." He rose to his feet, prodding the fire. "Not just peace in the land." He pointed across the flames upon my own chest. "Peace that resides there, within you." He then tapped his faculty. "Then He helps up here. Which is the plight and carriage of our greatest war."

I nodded, not fully sympathetic in my acquiescence, yet grasping the allegory of it. "Upon my arrival this morn, you exclaimed that He is not angry and quick to resolve. You paint Him a light, generous, and a sweet King. Still your actions of yesterday might..." I tossed about to apprehend the most scrupulous lexeme. "Well, be excused as the dodlings of any man within that self-same posture. A lovely lass...well a woman, nonetheless, upon you in such a fashion as to have a gracious night. Common is such a thing. Yet you frustrate yourself with malfeasance and dishonor. I am to judge because, as you know, I was present within the occasion and an attestant to all that was to befall. During and as well as post your egression." His smile ne'er ceased upon that daft face. I was hard-pressed to find a fault within his pietisticness.

"Thou hast a point with which your allocution doth go on?" He spoke, banterless.

He was not besmirched or tripped by my inquest. "I do eschew your reasoning, but not your loyalty. Admirable, notwithstanding I cannot accord with it." I stood to prepare my pallet. Of a truth, I worried it would become a problem to my quest more than I cared of his frailties. He remained sitting and silent. A mad beam ne'er relinquished his mug.

As I came to my feet, I descried a company of lights farther along the highway. "Behold, we are not far off the coterminous village."

He rose from the stump he perched upon and turned to witness. "Aye. Not far. The morn shall present a pleasant outset. Perhaps a hearty breakfast awaits us there."

◆　◆　◆

As it is with each day, the sun rose and forced the somber upon itself; and the epoch was begun. Now in the light, I marked the locale of the lights from the night anteriorly. The edifice that did correlate was not one of great nobility. It was barely there at all.

Caducus agreed. "I cannot see that it be as much as the lights of which we gazed upon last eve."

We broke camp and lade our mounts. Was a short constitutional to such as where the lights were. A grand disappointment, 'twas indeed. A simple, rutty structure 20 cubits width and half such deep. Albeit the thing looked as a stand meant to sell the goods of the day. Yet, nary a soul about it. The doors remained open, yet no one or no thing upon the walls, the counter, or the floor for that matter. "'Tis an odd thing, of a certain." I remarked.

"Indeed. Much is missing." Caducus agreed.

We cast about within to find not even the plainest of proof that any lived there or had been upon the premises of late. We yet found our questions only rising. The house was empty and undivided, old and fusty. Another back door stood open. "'Tis a queer and regal thing. To have had such a bright shine upon the night and dead still here, now." Caducus spoke.

"Queer indeed. Too greatly of such." I feared something sinister. "Do you feel as though there are eyes upon us? Here, now?"

Caducus glanced about as though he could find the spy. Upon the wall that which we entered there was yet a door that egressed to the front. Yet, I had failed to see another way in when we crossed the threshold. Such the mystery came upon dear

Caducus at the instant as upon myself. I stepped to the front to ensure our discovery. I looked back at my companion. "Nay. 'Tis a ruse." We both approached it, yanking our arming. As we did draw near, the door moved a slight. A stubby-fingered hand slid out from behind it. It ceased and gripped the plank. I poked the door with my blade. "What manner of forbidden magic is this?" I demanded.

"Please, oh please." A weak voice called out. "'Tis nothing of the sort, m'lord. A simple game. Nothing more."

"Show yourself. Elst I shall drive the door and you with it." I spoke as I assumed I would do. Though I had no intentions of such. As I guarded the door from off to me own side, Caducus reached from behind and snatched it to a wide open gaping. There, a top a dropping staircase, stood a great and tiny man. He was dressed as the famed leprechauns, in all green and brown. Hair as though he'd been within Rubropontem and was caught by one of the painters. Ears pointed and freckles enough to coat the snout of a dozen young giddy schoolgirls.

He bundled his arms up to protect himself from us, turning his noggin and squeezing his wee eyes shut tight. "M'lords, please. Do not hurt me."

Whilst I was enthralled with the little beast before me, Caducus pointed to the staircase upon the rear of him. "'Tis an odd thing that. Drops a might fast and sharp. A trick of the mind." He pointed at the door of which we entered. We both looked over and past the midget to see a light of some sort down below.

"What is this, little man?" He looked up at me. For just the briefest moment, I saw scheming in his eyes, yet deliberated no more of it. He smiled, as an innocent would when seeking a pleasing master's reply.

"'Tisn't an evil thing. A place. One of wonder and amusement. Not of any harm or pain. One of resort and pleasure. We call it the Bravio." He smiled, inviting. "A varius. For games. Please, m'lords, join me and a frore mead. Aye, and more. As agreeable food."

"It is a bit early for a mead." I pointed out. 'Twas not even warm enough to desire such, but I was hoping upon a bite.

"I believe we should move on, dear Miratus." The mystic King-worshiper spoke.

I looked upon him. "I am hungry, my friend. We can feed our stomachs for the day to come and then depart. None the less replete." I looked down upon the scamp there in the door. "Besides, I do not fear what a mere minikin could do. Me father's sword is of one and the same height."

"What is there to fear from myself? I cannot maul the mite. I am innocent." The leprechaun exclaimed.

"Aye. Innocent like Antitheus." Caducus said.

The small creature bowed. "I am Aleo. Your host. Please join us." He stepped aside, ignoring the comment of my companion, and invited us down. I went, hungry 'til me own gut spoke ill of me. 'Twas a powerful smell I found wafting up the strange, round about staircase. Powerful and delicious. What awaited myself was unknown, but I would desist the fear that poor Caducus lived in.

I felt the movement above me and realized that He had, despite his misgivings, joined me upon the steps. "Smell that, my friend?"

"Aye, but 'tis your hide that drives me down this awful and unexplainable hole."

"I need not your protection. A simple house, a miniature people. I can withstand whatever evil they devise." It was enough that I knew my need for him upon this wayward quest, but I would not have it that he knew as well.

The room we came into was as the outdoors, it was such in size. Table and chair of every sort. As to the proof of it all, the bounding size of it all was bare adequate for the people who occupied the bowels of this hole. Of every age, of every size. Man and woman alike. Indeed, a varius. I had ne'er been too much to game me own coin. I had ne'er had enough to go within the confines of such a place. I had found it to be something of kings and noblemen. Yet a place as this would cause reconsiderations in the staunchest decisions.

Glaring about as whimpering school boys, Caducus and I stood to take in the bustle and commotion, and the little man tapped me upon my legging. "The food is this way. I will show you. We have much to offer." Upon the tiny end of the luck we traipsed. My taste and appetite salivating for food, yet a tugging at me came as I heard from throughout the room, more and more, the sound of prizes begotten.

We followed to the farthest end of the great hall. There the meals were being served. And the victuals were both generous and wonderful. We sat and ate, watching the crowd of players. There were no maidens to serve. All seemed to be of the leprechaun. They weren'tst the twinage. But none were that were not cadre other than the little ones. There seemed many.

Was a bit and we were extravagantly imbued. More food than either of us had taken in for some time. Aleo came to see if we had enough. "Yes, my small friend. That was not only of great piquancy, but a generous fare as well." I patted my stomach. "And what upon do we owe thee for such a meal?"

"My friend, please. Your fare was upon me ownself. We love knights. 'Tis a pleasure to serve those who serve and risk the greatest for those who cannot." He smiled as he patted the table in front of us. He then pointed to the games before us. "Take some time and enjoy yourself."

I stood to my feet. "You are most kind, sir." I was not even aware of whose kingdom we were in. *Miles militis quod.* A knight is a knight wherest he be.

Caducus stood and bowed towards our host. "We are gracious upon your generosity." Aleo walked away without acknowledging the bow, nearly as though he was not there. He looked confused.

I roared in laughter. "You, the non-believer, Cad, my friend. Come. Let us repay their hospitality with a small gaming." I pointed to the tables about the room.

"'Tisn't a game. Call it as it is, and let us be about our way." He insisted. He really was a cad.

"Please, you are being indecorous. We shan't be long. And, mayhaps, a few coin heavier upon our exodus." It was a light thing that required not the wit or grasp to understand. They have granted us a vast banquet that would hold our feables the whole day. We respond in kind by forfeiting a few pence. Expectations of winning were ne'er real. But who's to say?

He did not agree. Of which I expected no less. Yet he did not leave. "If thou were to wait with our mounts, I do promise to not stay more than the loss of, say, five pence."

"No. The boys will remain. They are sure footed and most loyal. I will stay with you for now." He oathed unto me.

"Then, so be it. Let us find a table to give it up." I took to the crowd.

I knew the faintest of the games. Yet I charged in among them as though I was the greatest of gamblers within the house. 'Twas in the approach, I was of certain. Of a truth, I knew one game: Modin. Not even a well-known tryst but was my thin knowledge, still. Not a moment into my search and the Modin table sat before me. The tri-spinner, the catch, the die. They were there, and I sat upon my mini-quest to lose the five pence.

Me plans were left, moments later, behind. Dusted and lonely as my spinning became incomprehensible. Soon I was at 100 pence. The Modin spinner loved my hand upon it. Then I was at 200. Then more. The noise of all became beyond anything I had experienced. My dear Caducus, once the great naysayer to this game, now rooted me on. As did the large crowd that had pushed into my table. Yes, it was *my* table now.

Soon I had the coin to buy anything I wanted. I felt as likely to be floating above the ground as to be under it. Suddenly I had over a thousand pence. It was more than I have ever been paid as a knight. Then I doubled it. And again. Me pile of coin was such I could own the whole of Patrice. All the way unto Fastus' bridge.

I looked about the table and saw faces I'd yet to know. And likely would ne'er. Among them that of the little Aleo. He laughed and giggled. His was the losing end, yet seemed as happy for myself as any other.

I continued to lay all I had to the fate of the spinner. Nearly 4,000 pence, I lay upon one final spin. It twirled, it caught the die, it flew heavenward, it landed. Neither within my square or upon me number. And like that, all I had come to have, was gone. In a moment the crowd was gone. The cheering died away. I stood alone except for that travel companion, Caducus.

"'Tweren't yours to start. There is no loss but those five pence for your meal." He said. A moment before I was as wealthy as the lords and nobles. He brought it so low. I spun upon and swung me fist. To which he deftly was missed.

"Wait. Wait, my friends." Aleo raised his hands to stop us. "'Tisn't all lost. No, not for a knight of your obvious caliber." He stepped between us. I fear now I would have beaten him. And, would have regretted it for much to come.

"Explain, my little friend." I said.

"You know what credit is, sir knight?" He said, looking up at me.

"Of course. I am no lily." I remarked.

"Credit to you, my friend. Up to a thousand pence, since you were more twice that." The tiny thing had raised his hands in the air as though he'd offered the world unto me. It took but a frightfully brusque juncture for me to grasp a shaky, yet worthy rationale in his offer.

"Proceed, my good man." I exclaimed. "*Tu solum vivis unum tempus*! Chance be what it may!"

"Miratus? Do not be such daft. 'Tis a fool's choice!" Caducus declared. "You've not the time to figure the debt."

I looked upon him. His equitable ratiocination notwithstanding, my look betokened a strong invitation to remain incoherent. He did step back, yet unwillingly. Aleo offered the die, and I began again.

As before, I did magnificent. Die and the spinner alike played to me own favor. Cagey, I refused to unload the whole of the sum. Soon, my pile of pence amounted to nearly 1,500. 'Twas an amazing thing to realize.

Foolishness did, however, indeed, reign upon me. Because of my thinking to not bid me entirety, I began to lose in smaller fragments. I bet less, I lost less. I looked at the small fortune to which I had accumulated. It had descended nether to just a mere over 400. I felt a place that I should cease. And announced it as such.

Entangled in it all, I neglected one item of great import. "Well, that 'tis indeed a difficult ending, my friend." I found the little *gnome malum* at my elbow. "Might I inquire as to your form of payment?" He catechized.

I was fully dumbfounded and, no doubt, it was blatant upon me visage. The commons credit had been 1,000. For which I had fatuously and avericely fell upon. Now it was that I had in my possession 410 pence, yet for which I owed 1,000 pence. I graciously handed which I had to the little man. One which I would have no dilemma in defeating. Though I had no means by which to ensure it, I offered my word. "I shall return within a fortnight to repay the remaining sum. 'Tis upon my word as a knight! *Quia sermo meus miles!*"

I watched my consort from the edge of the crowd beginning to gather. I had no idea how true a friend he were to become. I saw his hand cover the hilt of his sword. Caducus stood keen to fight, with me, our way to our mounts and on to me quest. Ours, that be.

"'Tis a truer thing than I to take thee at thy word, my friend. Yet, this enterprise..." He raised his minnowie arms to indicate the whole of the buried varius. "This, it is not mine the which to allow such an offer. My lord, Lucrum, he demands a proper and standard arrangement. Credit is a simple offering to just a few habitué. Still, payment is guerdon upon cessation of the game."

"If thou wouldst return the remaining credit, I shall play to regain what I owe." I proffered the solution.

"Nay, my inproficient knight. The odds are not to your favor now." He refused. "I must needs remittance." He glanced at the coin in his hand and looked back up to myself. "'Tis 590 pence now. Accrual will inaugurate forthwith."

"If it were within me to bestow such a sum to you now, such would have I used to begin with and not thy credit *ludus*, to which you found me the fool and hoodwinked me thereof." I spoke downward to him. I had yet to espy any that worked within the hovel that were to be able to best myself alone. Much less I and my companion.

His face conspicuously reddened. "Thou, sir, mistake thyself. None were the moments of duress upon your person. Judgment were all within your very own bridle." I rested my hand upon my hilt as Caducus had. The leprechaun clearly saw it and backed hence.

For how long the varius had been in place was unknown to either myself or that of Caducus. We had ne'er traveled the Arbitrium Highway before. Yet convinced were myself that I could have my way by virtue of sword. Fancied I that they had ne'er had such fray within the confines of that place. My intimidation to be of that which would overcome him because of his diminutive size. 'Twas another step of foolishness upon my part.

The varius endured in a boisterous clamor from the tick of our arrival. Now suppressed as a den of serpents, the conflict had garnered the attention of all bettors and bettees alike. "Lacertus!" The meager brute bellowed.

I withdrew my armament a mere hands-breadth. To ensure that me opponent, no doubt this Lacertus, knew upon arrival that my intent was sure. The cluster that had come near about to distinguish the proceedings, now pushed back upon themselves. Aleo blended among them, virtually disappearing. None less than seconds passed and a span seemed clear before me. Caducus briskly at my side. "'Tis no need to mention again that which you have thus once proclaimed." We stood side by side as the crowd continued to widen the gap. Like a prince or great royalty was come upon the floor before us.

"I am certain there is little need." He spoke as he pulled his sword from its scabbard. "*Sic ego dixi vobis*. Lessons best learned are learned by folly."

I pulled me own glaive loose. "I aforesaid you could remain unexpressed. 'Twas plain." I grinned as though all was well. "Perchance we remain ourselves and upright, quench the grave, you may rail at me as thou desires."

We faced what was to come upon us with bravery. *Iuncta*, side by side. Watching the distant bulwark of the chamber. Upon my thoughts were the memory of Fastus. My knowledge of the old tongue searched. Lacertus. The name meant something. All names do. "The name, Lacertus...can you recall the meaning?" I asked Caducus.

"No. Yet it does mean something. As did Fastus." He glimpsed to me. "I know it, but my recollection is vague."

Frequenters continued to spread forth and the space between grew exponentially. The liberty opened with a few game tables in the center. They were suddenly swallowed up by the floor; and we remained there, a great gap before us. I looked to the stairs that which we entered the varius proper. A need to run over-came me. Caducus saw the direction of my gaze.

He looked there as well. "'Twould be impossible, *amicus meus*. The crowd doth prevent that departure." Indeed, the people had moved as one back in the duo proclivity. Who appeared as ready for the battle to ensue as any. "They seek the fight."

From within the far wall broke a noise of terror that silenced what bantam mumbling still endured. A crumbling of the rock wall began. Rock and soil fell as a double-sided door opened. It reached the high ceiling for its quantity. From the darkness that reigned within, a shadowy figure emerged. It was near the height of the door. A figure garbed in a long mantle. And led by a foursome of monster hounds. As I had heard of, but scarce believed.

"Master Lacertus." I heard the voice of Aleo from the crowd. "These knights have failed to present theirs what is due thou." As small as Aleo was, were the giant called Lacertus. Was a truety the hounds that Lacertus reined were larger than Aleo.

"'Tis a grand time to run, but where so?" Caducus leaned into me.

"Yea." I looked the opposite of the round stairs to where the hall concluded and where our meal had been consumed. "Think thou they've a back way?" I asked.

He queried the end of the room with his glances, hardly moving his eyes from the beast approaching. "Impossible to know. Likely a need for one, with all the food prepared herein."

The creature beneath the great robe stopped. It was a measly five cubits or less upon us. The monster dogs upon their leashes writhed and yanked to be loose. They were the means of sleeplessness, nightmarish at their best. "Ye hounds of hell..." I breathed.

"Not, I do think. But their cousins, nonetheless." Caducus enjoined.

I looked about the room to our left. 'Twas filled with people and games. Still most of both were to the right.

"A great and powerful lizard." Caducus spoke.

The room of people had begun to murmur. Bets aplenty of our fate. It was now a bit difficult to hear as those murmurings were filled with echo from the vaulted ceiling. It was that I could not understand him. "A wizard?" I replied. Then I saw the massive arms that pointed towards us from the robe of Lacertus. They were covered upon with drawing. The creature, which we now believed to be a mere mortal (and yet a man) was tattooed to appear as a lizard. As though great scales were upon all his skin.

"Lacertus. The legendary name of a great and powerful lizard." He re-asserted.

"Did such a monster truly exist, or 'tis this the only extent of it?" I nearly shouted to ensure he heard me.

He looked at myself. "You can be a fool when thou desires, can you not." He did not a question put to me. 'Twas a fact he alluded. I wanted to quarrel him on the matter, but the hounds were a bit more pressing.

Indeed, they were much closer than Lacertus. They were all of the same birthing. Black, substantial, and, as difficult as it seemed, far more teeth than their vast mouths should hold. Slime and gruel slithered from their gaping cavities. Equally large those as well. They wailed and howled to be set free and come upon us. Thankfully, the giant man of many marks held them back. 'Twas his right that pointed to us and his left that restrained the mongrels. From beneath the cover of his murky hood, his voice cast as a deep, guttural ache sounded by demons and trolls. And knew the sound of the trolls, I did. "Thou humble creatures dare to challenge the House of Lucrum? Upon us, it may ne'er be said that we would bring suffering upon an innocent. I will give you the one chance to pay the games as thou dost owe. Now."

"Pardon, my good sir. Do you have upon your person the sum of 590 pence?" I gingerly asked my companion.

"My most humble regrets, kind sir." Mocking me as much as I mocked the mammoth before us. "Not a pence to me name."

"As I surmised." I looked about the room. My mind wandered just a bit at the sight of what was clearly some kind of exit. Even if only wherefore to the kitchen. *Must*, my heart spoke, *be a rear egress there.* "As I go, thee go. And fast." I added, for his ears only.

"Aye. I am ready." He countered.

I put me sword to the ground. The tip of the blade sat edge upward a bare hands-breadth from the closest cur. It would seem a surrender on my part. The knight exemplar, that my companion was, saw post haste me plan. I glanced upon his smile as his blade joined mine, a scant farther from the chin of the second hound. I looked upon the man-lizard before us. "My lord." I spoke in fraudulent acquiescence. "I beg your forgiveness. 'Twas a fool-hearted endeavor on my behalf to scrounge up the coinage to makest me life better. I've the eleven children, me wife of greediness likest not known till now, and the mother-in-law with which to contend and work duly for. Is there a simple understanding that shall be for myself?" Caducus stood at my side. He flinched not a wink, yet I knew he'd come upon the giggles at my earnest, albeit spurious, plea.

"You are a fool if thou thinkest a moment that your petition is succumbing to me. You have been given your chance." His arm returned to his side. He seemed particularly final about the matter.

"Well, then. I have made me appeal. Askance upon forgiveness." I bowed deeply. Caducus mimicking myself. "Thou has forced my minimal response." Upon the last word, I nudge me crony and our swords rose as one, slicing up and through the bottom jaws of the nearest two hounds. Though we yet had the two succeeding to contend with, those first dropped in their place, effusively opened and abundantly dead.

The savage act brought the crowd to a shaken silence. Beast-man, Lacertus, as well, was persuaded into dumbness. Brief though this placidity may be, we moved, not waiting upon those within the cavernous hall to stir from their transfixion.

I dug my sword point into the wood floor, ancillary to my vaulting upon the first game counter. Upon it, running across, upon the next. One more and I found the crowd to be more than I could simply leap. My sword about and they retreated upon themselves. One bold one, some form of a knight who sought the favor of the house, challenged myself. He braced his rapier to me. Caducus, at my nearest breech, came around with great speed from the table he was upon, crossing the brave foe's armature hard. He drove the point down and piled his weight upon him proper and to the floor. I pulled him up, and we carried onward at the kitchen door.

Inside infantine moment that had passed, yon Lacertus had released the lingering hounds to be at us. I believe they had whimpered at the foremost that now lay corpses upon the floor. Which no doubt fed to their angst of Caducus and myself. We refused to swivel upon the aft and careened about the gamblers and games, ambitiously pointed upon the target of escape. Wistfully through the canteen.

We succumbed the eatery tables, bounding inelegantly as two foxes twixt tails tied, upon, over, around, and purposefully through to the door that parted the galley and the varius. In which none were scarcely aware of the commotion amongst the games. Such was that our entrance took all cooking, bussing, and serving at great wonderment. Dishes were dropped. Utensils as well.

The kitchen looked none from any other. We charged for the doors in the back. The screams and the snarls of the two hounds not a hand's toss from upon us. The meal cadre shirked, shifted, and swerved from us as we strived to continue our evasion. All the same as the host, freckled, tiny, red haired, and in green, moved left and right, amazingly deft upon counters, tables, and even a grand stove. Of which just the second I did hope 'twas not lit. The doors in the back arrived, and we chose. That which was the storage first, then back to the other. As we did, I spied those mongrels bursting upon the scullery entrance. Their keen monster eyes picking us from the now unsettled room.

The second door was exactly as we had hoped. A brief length of steps to ground above and we found ourselves within another building. I could hear the noise of equine and other animals. The varius' stable. Filled up, no doubt, of the patrons' own transports. A barn as a maze and a difficult time we had trying to exit. None were about to tend. Abate us, the dogs charged the doors below. "They are near through. Another shall open that door and they should be upon us." I held.

We parted to locate the way out from the vast keep. A scant breath and Caducus called he'd found it. Upon the egress we found ourselves within a forest, not the bare hillside that the shack sat upon. We cast about to find a trail that led back towards the Arbitrium. Once there, we saw the shack that we had entered through was back along the road some distance north. In minutes we had our steeds and, near breathless, mounted. It was upon us both to readily return to the way south. A trifling chortle at it all and we skirted back upon the Highway.

As we came upon the trail we had ascended, we looked down it. There, coming at a full run, were the two remaining mongrels. Longwise and Gallant were up to it as we spurred them into a run. The Mutts of Lacertus gave chase. Much faster than I suspected they even could.

It was yet another five miles before we slowed, resting in the assurance that the hounds were gone from sight and unable to give further chase. The horses were game, but we slowed them to rest.

"'Twas a place I shan't miss." Caducus spoke, a smile upon him. And a glance back or two.

"Nor I, my friend." I looked at him. His lot was not with me, yet he had set our friendship within stone. "You did risk much for my foolishness. I am forever grateful."

"I've had more done for me. There were no other way I could." He nodded. He reined up and looked back upon the trail, again. "Beasts are from sight, but me thinks not lost. Merely slower."

Stopping as well, I joined him in a look north. "'Twill be ever so until they lay as their brothers. I would ne'er cease upon the quest of one who took any of family from me." I turned back upon the south and resumed.

**"For the love of money is the root of all kinds of evil,
for which some have strayed from the faith in their greediness,
and pierced themselves through with many sorrows."
1 Timothy 6:10**

Chapter 6
Alium

The way before us was on and on. We wandered about the mountains. Our rations ran low, we trapped meat. There was much fruit along the paths. And that is what lay before us often, naught but a trail. We passed other travelers. Often staying with strangers in customary camps. We learned of the lives we two had. He had spent as little time upon quests as I had. Though he spoke freely of his errs and hardships, I remained as forbidding as I could. I feared we'd battle one another one day, and he'd have the advantage. He did not insist; I kept silent oftener as did he.

I secretly pulled my map from the satchel to ensure I was still upon the quest. We watched for Juxta Iter, the next village with which we'd come to. I asked another pilgrim as we passed, and he gathered we'd be a day out. That last night we spent in the wilderness before Juxta Iter, we were alone. We had found a bare corner of ground up a short rise from the highway. We were still concerned of the hounds. Though a number of days had passed, we were both of a certain that we had heard the curs howling throughout the journey. We had even warned a few traveling the other way. As domestic beasts, we indeed hoped they were unlikely to devour just anyone on their passage to catch us.

We sat upon logs drug into our camp. "'Tis a thing we will have to do. I pray it does not take us much from the way." I spoke.

"You do mean the hounds?" Caducus asked of me.

"Indeed. Likely we will have to hunt down the mutts. Us or them. They do not appear to have left off. I am certain they are that which bays upon the dark as a wolf, yet not a wolf." I posted further.

"True, the howl is wrong for a wolf. It is they. And, yes, 'tis inevitable." He agreed.

As if the mongrels knew the moment where with we'd be about them in our confab, we listened upon the wind of a long, guttural moan. A moment passed, as we heeded the wail of a second, distinct cry. "Indeed."

The distance betwixt the howls and our own camp was sufficient that we were of no concern. Not for the night, at still. Their approach would abate the rift before long but for us to spend a significant part of the day at a run or speedy gait. "They shall follow us into the village." Caducus put to me.

"Yes. We should plan to deal with them on the morrow." I looked in the direction of the howls. Dead branch in hand, I spread the fire to die off. It was time to find my pallet. We both lay with sword in hand and one eye upon the trail below us.

◆ ◆ ◆

Morning found us upon the highway again south near day. We'd gone scarce a bit when Caducus stopped and pointed in the dirt at the foot of Gallant. "Our pursuants were upon us and past." I looked to the ground and saw, most present and obvious, the large sign of a hound's foot. They had somehow missed us passing forth in the night.

"'Tis a blessing of ours they did not smell our deviation to the hillside. They'd have been upon us within our slumber." I said.

"Indeed." He glanced about. "The markings are spread apart. They happened upon here in a hurry. A strong gait."

"Yes. As though on something more specific." I remained to ferret the pathway.

"Nothing more." Caducus said. I agreed, and we rambled on. "Must favor the tracks. I know not of their scheming, if they are of the mind to trap us."

"Me notion is they are heedless to us now. No doubt still intent upon our demise, yet beyond us somehow." I declared. Caducus nodded in agreement, and we carried forward.

'Twas a scant hour hence, post a watchful eye, we perceived a scream from before us. We looked upon one another, then stirred our mounts to a strong gait. With path before us winding and rough, we saw the frantic race of a straggling mount, without a rider, charging at us, then past. The ground about was uphill to our right and a drop to the left. Both covered with attendant and sparse trees. A variety of oak and cedar and spruce. Some bush and shrub. Yon trail turned sharply in upon an egress of the mountain to our right and back out. As it did so, I could hear the beasts growling. Another turn and we fell upon them.

A traveler and his serf had been taken by surprise and tossed by the great beasts. Within the dim light of the varius, I had forgotten the size of these monsters. 'Twas a bit uncommon to see affluent travel in such fashion. And affluent he were for none but such owned a serf. He, nonetheless, was the first to succumb to the terrors as he was bloodied and lay still upon the ground there. The serf, of a young age, and typical of a muliebrous chattel, had muddled her way up a few branches of an ancient and barren tree.

Determined as the one was to attain her, it would succeed in short. The other was occupied upon the now carcass of the man.

We simultaneously slid from our steeds, swords already drawn, and charged the beasts, hereforeto thought of life or limb. *Est qui sumus*, 'tis who we are. Our arrival was not sly by any means. The creatures both turned from that which had their attention and looked, thus, upon us. It was a scant second or two before recognition came upon them, and they drove at us.

These two wast more prepared than that of their brothers. A simplistic move of the blade was not enough. One who has been taught the parry and thrust shouldst understand the mere trouble of a hound. Even that as large as these. But not so. We found a genuine trouble of these two. Contrary to their cadaverous duo kin, these were not upon a rein, held in check. They dodged our sword near effortlessly. Which put the defense quickly upon ourselves. Moments of this became exhausting.

"'Tis a suffering of such. We must needs alter our tactics, my friend; or we shall soon be so much hound fodder." I cast out to Caducus. Of whom was a handful as much as mine. I nodded at the corpse that lay nearby. "As he is now."

"Thou dost solicit such a proposal grand for certain." He fought on. "Please, me companion of hypothesis, elucidate myself."

I roared a noise of intimidation. Which appeared half in alarm and half in jovial caterwauling. "Arrrrggggghhhhh!" It served little. The mutt paused only the briefest of seconds. "I've nothing." I glanced at him as he swung at the monster he fought upon. "And, thou?"

"'Tis not a fight of the commoner knight. Of which I am. They are as big as we and quicker." He breathed and swung again. "Were they of the sword, we'd long be dead, my friend."

It was unnecessary to reply for he knew my affairs as I knew his. A swing and the sword tip met the mark upon the side of me own prodigium's scalp. A victory for sure, yet the thing merely rolled and came again. The creature was made of leather thick like the wall of a castle. "I cannot pierce the cursed brute!"

"Indeed. I have laid the edge upon now many times. They are demonic." He responded.

The hound I fought with became wary as I swung upon it. He stepped to the breech and jumped upon me. The paltry mail I wore beneath my smock kept a stray tooth of tremendous point from running me through. I pushed off and found meself upon the ground, at his mercy. He towered me by a few hand-breadths with me upon the dirt. I looked up as he approached.

Remembering the soft tissue of the previous brother's nether, I knew there I could pierce this brazen hide. It was the fate of the monster to die as his kin had done so. My hand upon my sword lay flat on the ground. I slid my body back hence, keeping the sword outward. He was of great perception for that of a mongrel hound. Yet he was a dull wit as to the obvious. His approach brought him undeviatlingly over the end of my sword. I brought it straight up as I had in the varius with the other, yet pointedly into the shoddy of his neck and jaw. As his brother had, he dropped, expired upon impingement.

I rose to discern Caducus' parley continuing with that which still lived. The silence in my quarter caused them both to look. The hound turned on me and began a swift charge. The mongrel's angst to me was such that he lost complete concern of me fellow knight. Believing the back of the neck to be of similar skin, Caducus drove his sword such deep within. I cannot say if a dog would be want to show remorse or surprise, but it did such appear to be as this last fell at the hands of my compeer.

"Let us ne'er perpetrate a varius again." I suggested.

Caducus looked in surprise. "Yet, my friend, "'tis a place of wonder."" He mocked Aleo.

"Come on down, my youngster. You are safe now." He said to the girl in the tree.

I concerned myself with her. Were she to the man whom was most dead upon the ground, she now belonged to his heir. "You are the property of this man?" I asked "A serf?"

Caducus looked at me, speaking before the child could respond. "Why do you assume her to be a serf? What of her makes a slave so obvious?"

I looked at him. *He is indeed advena*, I thought to myself. "You are new to these realms. I understand." I pointed at the young maiden. "Her dark skin. They are not of our citizenry. Serfs. She is his property."

The girl, for that was mostly what she was, just a child, made it upon the ground and went to the man. "M'lords. As gracious as he was, I am to you. Me thanks you of your bravery."

"You speak?" I exclaimed. "'Tis a fool's gallantry to teach a serf to grunt in such elegance. Be quiet." She fell silent. She wore simpleton clothes. The age of near adult, healthy. Her master made certain she was tended well. But, beyond all else, she was vassal first.

"'Tis a horrible deed. To be of service lacking choice. I could not imagine it." Caducus spoke. From his own deficiency I imagine most. "What is your name, child?"

She looked to me. I had the authority she needed. It was her nature grown as a slave to recognize the one who was in charge. I nodded, implying she may respond. She looked back at Caducus. "I am called Alium."

"From whence thou comes?" I asked the slave.

"Inlitora. To the south. We were on our way unto..."

"'Tis enough, serf!" I interrupted. "Your travel is nothing to us. You belong to the heir, whoever that is." I found my way back to Longwise and took his bridle. "Be on your way to Inlitora. We shall dispense with your master." I took my steed and found a nearby log to drape his reins to.

"Wait, Alium." Caducus raised his hand.

"Caducus, my friend. Upon this all lies an orderliness. It was established upon lore, such was the time ago." I plead. "Let us be on our way." I pointed to the dead there in the road. "A hole, a body. Let us be about it."

"A moment, friend. She is but a lass. Far too young to travel alone. Is it not enough that she has experienced such a terror? We cannot leave her to the wilds of neither the land nor the miscreants she might encounter within the villages." He begged as though the slave were his own child.

"You are a fool. You know not what you engender yourself into. She is property! She is not yon's own sister." I raised my hands in disgust. "Do you not grasp this? 'Tis great trouble were we to be on with a slave of other's property."

"She is from Inlitora. Is it not yet before us? We can reasonably be the escort until we arrive at a parting." His words made sense, but I was wearied already from the morning's activities.

"Very well." I agreed. "Yet I do have some edicts of which you contain her in."

"Yes, go on, dear Miratus." He smiled as though a child having in upon itself.

"She shall eat of your own. Not mine." I declared.

"Indeed." He agreed again.

"You are fettered to her. She is your charge." I added.

"Yes, of course."

I looked at her. She knelt beside her old master. He was dressed fairly well and was not ethereal of size. "We shall assume the possessions upon his person. A traveler's right upon the duty of burial."

"You shall rob a dead man?" Caducus said in offense.

"'Tis the right of those who dig and bury." I pointed at the satchel and light pack I carried. "And upon us, I've no shovel. 'Twill be worth our labor, my friend."

He led Gallant to the log that Longwise stood to, then joined myself as we pulled rocks and dirt from the low side of the bank. A true hole to rest the well-heeled within took near an hour. We pulled him to it and found the pockets of the man empty. The girl seemed undiscerning, yet Caducus found the whole within the confines of great humor.

A dozen cubits farther on, the side dropped sheer a hundred down. We drug the hounds thereto and threw them over.

"Was your master poor?" I asked the young serf as we returned to our journey.

Without looking up at me upon Longwise, she spoke reservedly. "Nay, m'lord." She fought herself of drear. "Lord Opulentus 'twas his name. His pouch upon the mare was full."

I looked at Caducus, who, so daring, led his fair rather than make the serf walk alone. Once again, he fought to retain his laughter. It was a plain understanding that she spoke of the horse that had passed us most expeditiously a length back up the road. Of which was likely to be near a hundred furlongs away by now. Instinctively, I stopped Longwise and looked hindmost me up the road we'd just wound about. As though the mare would be there waiting our attention. She was not.

Young Alium had very little to offer in the way of speak. She was pithy about herself and her master. She replied to each inquiry, yea, but with as few words as she could muster. I demanded of her a reason. I feared she hid something important.

"You oaf." Caducus remarked. "You insisted she be quiet a bit back. Now you wish her to confer a symposium upon yourself? Please do adjudicate to which it is so that she, as much as I, might know what you fancy from her." Might as I thought to do so, he had a weighty contention. Nonetheless, I did not prefer to be told as an oaf.

I looked down upon the child. "Speak. Tell us the reason you and your master were about."

She dithered and faltered. 'Twas my fault, but I was averse to so say. Me own voice was harsh, and she became timorous of such. She convoked the bravura and spoke. "Our passage, we returned home. From Urbe Mortuos. The beasts caught us. My master fought bravely, commanding me to climb the tree." She wept. Upon her grief, I felt inclined to comfort her. Yet she was another man's slave.

"Urbe Mortuos?" Caducus asked. "I do not know this place."

"I have heard tale of it, but I fear I know nothing more." I replied.

Amongst her tears, Alium spoke. "'Tis the City of the Dead. Where some go to bury their esteemed and particulars."

I recalled more. "Yes, 'tis a strange place. A whole village of graves. I recall some prattle of it."

"Still nothing. Not a breath of it." Caducus spoke, bewildered. I looked at him, surprised by his ignorance. He smiled. "Means little. You have seen the breadth of my travel."

"Indeed." I glanced back to the child. "And didst your master bury a notable or attend the internment of another?"

She bowed her head. "'Twas that of his son. His only." Her whimper shook her.

Her genuine feelings for her master vexed me. With little time proximal to serfs or their generally wealthy owners, I had not within me to grasp the relationship betwixt them. She did not respond as I expected. She found no comfort to the loss of he which enslaved her. Which meant, as I felt, that he had valued her as greater than a simple possession. "Then thou goest home?"

"M'lord, yes. 'Twas our way back to Inlitora."

In me, my heart hurt for the child. And such a thing bothered myself. A slave was not equal to one who was as me. Though my day-to-day was a struggle and I possessed little, I was a knight of the realm and at the least, garnered the respect of citizens. She was far from it. Likely lesser in value to thus than Longwise or Gallant. Though my travels would take me to Inlitora. 'Twas on the map to the Chalice. Caducus knew not of that as I had spoken naught of it. Of which, he had also failed to enquire. I suspected we'd part foregoing then. Still, he had discerned that Inlitora was along the direction we traversed.

"We shall see thee home, child." Gallant's holder spoke, extending his arm about her.

"No we shan't. She is the property of another." I belied me own feelings on the matter. It being none of my carry on. Less so of his. He was blundering of it all. "It is well enough that she accompany us unto Juxta Iter. We shall leave her upon the constable there. 'Tis his task to secure her to him unto her abode. If need be, he shall send word to her legatee."

"She is but a thing unto you. Why dost you even concern yourself, then?" He insisted.

"You fool. That King of yours." I remarked, risking that which I feared most: a crossing of swords. Of such, yet, I felt he would not dare. Upon his own word. Yet it was not without concern. I knew within me it could not happen. I, myself, wouldn't as he had endangered his own breath and blood for the sake of myself. But I still concluded him a simpleton of his feebleminded thinking.

"Indeed!" He retorted. "My King. He would not be so maligned as to ignore this little one in her need. 'Tis a thing you could learn. I am not attached upon you. At your side to see you upon yours, I should remain. Yet not at the cause of a child in need. It may be that within this realm she is a chattel and of possession, but me own Kingdom resides always here." He pounded his own chest. "And within that Realm, she is a free and beautiful creature. Do as you wish, but this knight shall bring her to her own. At risk of life and limb!"

I forewent the fight and trudged on. He continued to morn with the serf. At length I asked who would resume her ownership. She stopped. And us with her. She looked at me, woeful. "At truth, m'lord, 'tis thee." I do believe my face paled.

"You are daft, child. How is that 'twould be I?"

She cowered to my command. I cared not. She did require a magnificent answer upon such utterance. "Dost thou always scream upon children? A father of such deserves nary an offspring." Caducus proclaimed.

"I have none and shan't before a wife." I replied.

"Huh?" He scoffed. "Shall be none that would acquiesce even upon the king's ransom to be such. You shall, indeed, be unfruitful unto death short a great vacillation within thy brainworks on a child." He was none patient with me, but remembered the child he so emphatically babbled on of. He looked at her. She did still cower to just a degree. "Explain, child?"

She stood up, but remained wary as she orated. "'Tis none to have me at the house in Inlitora. That which took my master, I am his."

"The beast took him." I entered.

"Yes, m'lord. And you took him." She bowed. "I am yours, m'lord." To which dear Caducus found, again, the moment of which to cackle enough to frighten the beasts of burden of which carried he and I. At least I as he remained upon his feet. As to the humor of it all, I saw none.

"Oh, master." He whooped. "The child is yours, no doubt."

"Nay." I retorted. "A fool's thought for that a mongrel could be in succession upon a slave's owning. What's more, such was as easily thy own sword." I nodded back at him.

Alium bowed deeply to the ground, remaining as she spoke to myself. "My humblest *mea culpa*, m'lord." She pointed from her bow there back towards Caducus. "He addressed that which had chased me."

"You suppose, slave, that within the pother of that uproar, you knew of that which beast was which? And, further suppose, that which I would take thy word on the matter?" I contended. Of which I knew there was little need. It was plain that she had little ambiguity on the purpose. 'Tis a much better status that she fall upon the mercy of Caducus than I. None the less, a man of wealth I was not and to own a serf was to tend to a serf. That required pence

I simply did not have. As such, me own wherewithal was all I had to tend upon me own needs.

Caducus, of a matter, saw this same argument that I fought within me. "She hasn't the slightest reason to bring a falsehood about. I believe that is plain." He smiled again. Such as I would have driven me gaunleted right within had it been another. "She is, indeed, yours."

I was as scandalized as one in my station could, precluding an outward reply. Brutishly, that were. Having not that which was me own thinking, I dug into Longwise; and we carried on farther ahead. 'Tis a terrible thing to have such a belly full, I couldst not propagate the concluding remark upon the discourse. Of which included a child of less than 15 years.

Our travel was separate for a time. I continued a dozen or more cubits forward, and they remained upon the ground. Indeed, as though betrayed for that mere serf, Caducus walked fierce Gallant while discoursing with young Alium as she were of the same footing as he. Or I, for that matter.

The route to Juxta Iter appeared farther along than I had come to understand. It is upon the longer journey that time and weariness lies unto our brains. Such was those to whom had passed the distance along upon our enquiries. And so it was that the day gained upon us; and we found the glow upon the horizon, dim and disappearing. A piddling trail to the inward and upward of the highway, led us to a paltry camp used oftimes by the marks of a blackened pit and trunks gathered about.

Little had been spoken of the ownership with which I now stood. 'Twasn't the thing I desired or grappled upon. Nor conducive to the quest I was upon and most desirous of. Yet, there within that small camp, I had to brave such and surmise its conclusion. We sat about a small flame, quiet. Alium remained off from the light of the fire. As a serf was meant to do. Her position was to be within my call, yet not within my vista. Caducus and I spoke not. I unsure of the moment, he not wishing to prod me, I believe, into the clear discord that would emerge. "She is yours." I spoke. It had been in me to do such. Caducus would, undoubtedly, seek a way to give her that of equal status to he and I, yet to tie her to him 'twas a better thing than to I.

In the faint light of that fire, I saw him grin as a cat upon a bucket of mice. "Nay, my friend. I will not accept." He distended his arms, yawning. "She is yours. At least until Juxta Iter." He rose to move to his pallet.

"I haven't the all in me to tend her." I begged upon his best. He snickered and rolled about to face away. *Indeed, until Juxta Iter,* I thought. *I shall find a few pence for her there. It shall irk my companion, but that is how our realm is here. 'Tisn't such as he likes, but he shall get along with it, fancy as he does or does not.* I veried that I should say as such to his own visage, yet I doubted it. Either one, sleep called unto me.

◆ ◆ ◆

'Twas a bit dark as I woke. With, of all things possible, the wafting of food upon me senses. And pleasant, at that. I rolled about to find a spit upon the fire, roasting such the smell as I noted. Suspecting me companion's foul cooking, I begged off. "'Tis dark still. Must you compel such upon me before the light of day even?"

"Ha, my friend. Look, 'tis but early. Yon hills lighten as we speak." He spoke from across the fire. I did look to his delight and found it dawning, red, yellow, and the scant royalty of blue. 'Twas a beautiful day to be, indeed. Nonetheless, the beauty of the day should be upon me whilest I was fully rested. I returned to my dankness. "Wake, you fool; or I shall eat of it completely. Save the cook, herself."

His words slipped in upon me, and I rose again. I recalled the serf and her presence. No doubt, she was gifted in the wares and needs of food. I looked again to the troublemaker across the blaze from me. "'Tis the serf cooking?"

"Nay. 'Twas Alium." He insisted. I believed he hated the word and further the thought. Such was this province.

"Prey not upon me boggled mind foregoing its awakeness. I still slumber." I rose to my feet, pushing the sleep slowly from me arms and legs. I sat, heretofore I rolled my pallet, upon the log beside the fire. I spoke in response to his stubbornness, not raising my eyes to meet his own. "She is a slave. She were born such. She shall die such. 'Tisn't upon you to change the casts of this time. Agreest or not." He remained silent.

I looked at the creature that spread across the fire. "'Tis a snake." I saw the smile again on my companion's face. "I've eaten the creatures before, knave. It cannot be worse than the rot gut you fed me days ago upon our exit from Rubropontem." At which we both laughed. "Yes, rot gut. Donkey stall fodder. Indeed."

"'Tis true." He agreed, grinning again. Such that would make the most meekest of men become suspicious of his wrongdoing. "But your dear child, here, she is not just better. She excels at the herb and season. How, I do not know. But you shall be mighty pleased upon her skills, my friend."

Though early morn, the surrounding forest was yet quite dark and foreboding. Much more so as a rustling emitted from it and something of size came at us. I quickly rose to me feet, fumbling upon my pallet and belongings for my sword. Of which I could not find. "'Tis Alium." He spoke such mildly as he nonchalantly pointed. Indeed, she stepped from the bushes to within the light of the flames. And, an armful of limbs and such. She bowed towards me most courtly.

"Alium, what is all this?" I demanded.

"M'lord, I was about the woods to gather for the fire and sometin' to add upon the asp." She slowly rose from the bow and placed the load within her arms upon the ground nearest the fire.

"Asp?" I demanded.

"Indeed, me lord." She pointed at the fire. "'Tis a succulent creature." She turned and walked towards the trail that we wound upon from the Arbitrium.

I remained looking at the asp. "The snake is most poisonous. Yet we plan upon breakfast with it?"

"Oh, me brutish soldier." Caducus mocked me.

"M'lord, I shall eat upon it first if thou dost require." Young Alium spoke from the dark where her pallet had been. She stepped closer as such I could see her face. "The poison is only within the head. Of which I buried in the woods yon." She pointed off to the dark brush of which she had just exited.

I was yet anxious of it all. "Very well." As I could, I returned to my pallet. Suddenly I was reminded that my sword was not to be found. I searched upon my possessions. Then upon my memory for the thing. *How dost one lose a full sword?* I thought. My pallet returned to Longwise, I continued to seek the weapon. I found a small limb and used it as a torch, casting about for it upon the ground out from where my pallet had lain.

A mere handbreadth from where my bedding had lain, I found a small puddle of blood. "Alium?" I nearly screamed. Were she to loose herself from me, she would be free. I deftly searched me providence and found nary a slice of injury that were not there before nightfall last.

"M'lord." She approached myself, my sword in her hands. I plucked it from her hands, pushing her back away. A brief examination I found it clean as it were the day I received it from me father. Cleaner still. And as sharp as it had e'er been.

"What is the meaning of this?" I pointed at the ground as the daylight began its real climb. "The blood, where from is it?"

"Thou nin. 'Tis the blood of the viper upon the spit." Caducus spoke up.

Upon examination of the two places, that of the snake cooking and the blood, I looked down at the child bowed before me. "Is this true, serf?"

"M'lord, I saw the creature moving upon you and your sword was near. I dulled it upon the dirt and thus was needs be to sharpen such. Forgive my insolence, my lord." She bowed even further. 'Twas a moment I shan't forget. It was not within me to believe anything but that which she had saved my fool life. And I did little to deserve such a thing.

She finished preparing our meal and it was, without me own doubt, the loveliest I'd ate since me own mother passed on. Though my heart fought me mind on the matter, my mouth was kinder and me heart was dealing with this change. As it should. I wondered to my own thought if I had been tugged upon into a way that might well have been wrong. Such would cause me questions to much.

I remained at peace in meself the morning on. Much pondering. And such I was hours later upon the highway once more when we were set upon. 'Twas indeed a fool thing as I led us to the ambush.

"Good morning to you then." A man of nigh my age. And then some, I suppose. He wore a raggedy buckskin coat and rags beneath. He slipped from behind a great oak cradling a rustic crossbow in his right arm, a finger resting upon the trigger. Warn the weapon was, but likely a strong agility with which he handled it. My hand landed upon the hilt of my sword forthwith. "Na, na...yon there in the trees me help be." I glanced back and forth to count another four arrows pointing from the thickest of brush. So much so, that the armed could scarcely be seen. The quarters we found ours within were cramped and gave us little to no room of which to move.

Unbeknownst to the two who trailed myself, they joined me as a small group, easily corralled. "Dost thou not see us?" I demanded. "We are knights. We shall take you five as though one."

The man laughed. "I have known many knights. They, mostly, are but as myself. Yet poorer. Hahaha..." I had little argument. "But thou, thou hast his own serf. Such a thing is not as common place." He pointed at Caducus.

"Pardon, m'lord. I belong to him." Alium pointed at myself. She referred to the scum highwayman as a lord.

I looked back to her. "'Tisn't a need to be polite upon the scrill here robbing us." I corrected the girl.

"Ahhh, no me lord. She is raist up rightly, aww boy." A voice came from one of those in the thicket. The brush hid them well, but the arrows poked about.

"Indeed. She'll fetch a nice pence within the city, she will. Nicely mannered and all." The leader said.

Caducus had drawn up a cubit to me sword hand. The youngster stopped betwixt us. She rested her hands upon the flanks of both Longwise and Gallant. "Can you not allow us on, dear sir? We have about a quest from our kings. Pray tell, dost thou truly wish upon us the errant of our mandates?" He pleaded. Certain of his true nature, his plea sounded a forgery. I watched to assure of his wariness.

"Such a fool would I be? You are not the wealth as we aim, but 'tis done what 'tis done. Unmount your beasts. Your all withal. And mosey on. We shall be happy to pull the arrows from your unmoving bodies, need it be." He motioned us from upon the horses.

"My good man..." Caducus began.

"'Tisn't the need to sparkle me eyes with your words, squire. Just get off your mount or perish as you are." He made about.

"Of course. But I would ask only the smallest of charity. Just this and we shall go with no words or dissensions." He begged. I watched him. It was that a conspirement was under the arm of his garment. His eyes bounced about as though he pointed with his brows.

"I shall not be so cordial, rapscallion indeed." I argued.

"Then you shall be through and through upon first." The gang leader spat at me.

"Nay. Please, me lord. One simple thing." Caducus continued to beg.

The master of the thieves took careful aim at my companion. "Speak before I let loose upon you."

"My lord, I thank thee." He motioned at me. "Take as thy will. Especially the serf. She has little value to us either. Take our sacks and the equine, indeed. Save us only the swords. 'Tis a much harder thing to replace. Only tools, yet costly to the knight with which has no pence. I to the front shall wish it upon thee only good. And, my fool squire to his rear, always and only, I vow upon thee a good repose."

"What fool babbling you doth go on about?" The thief looked about at the others in his group. I did not understand the noise dear Caducus went on with either. "Ummm..." Caducus clearly wished to create perplexity.

I sharpened on the locations he spoke. He told of my good intended from me rear. I glanced at the arrow with which protruded from the thicket nearest my rear. It pointed upon me. I looked about to as not appear me eyes upon it, but the arrow to me hinder did not move about as the one that was to me front and left did. Indeed, 'twas a prop!

"Be that as such, I am not the fool thou believest I am. Get from your mounts or die in the way of it." The man demanded.

I glanced upon my wily companion and nodded enough that he saw. We descended the steeds, landing both to the breech of the young serf. He to the left, I to the right. In a moment he placed her hands upon the pommels of our meager saddles. He was cagey, undoubtedly. He motioned her to hang on and, while in the cover of the horses, told me to slap Longwise. We did as one, and she took strongly upon the pommels. The sudden commotion threw our assailant off as his arrow flew upwardly and harmless.

In a moment, Alium was clear of danger; and we swung our arms about. Indeed, there was but the two in the brush, forward to myself and rear upon him. With which we had dispatched readily and directly. I looked about to find the poor fellows' miscreant chief was long about the road ahead, as well his feet could carry him such. He looked back upon us. Fearing his life, he ran upon a trailhead he'd no doubt hidden his own horse within. At his approach, Longwise, young Alium mounted and trudging him on, charged the wayward thief and knocked him asunder. The blow threw him to a large cedar trunk and removed his might to prolong his amble.

We fetched their horses up to the highway and laid the two that had met their demise 'cross their own. The knave provocateur that led the rabble, we tied snug and reined his horse for him. "It shall be the rocks or worse for thou," said I, a nasty grin upon me face.

"Ha, nay you, fool. If thou takest me unto Juxta Iter, it will be a holiday for me." He leaned just enough to keep his abode within his inutile pillion. "Even the constable is me cousin."

"Why then, your kinsman shall have you." Caducus belted. "'Tis not a concern upon that time. As now, wayward bandit, be thou still or you shall arrive as your partners shall." He pointed at the two dead bodies upon the other horses.

"Yes, there be that..." He conceded.

◆ ◆ ◆

Within the bellows of my heart, I fought. I fought the upbringings of myself and those about me. That which I knew to be true now battled with that I had come to understand. 'Twas much that I now questioned as to right and to wrong. Within me newest friend roared the heart of a lion. Surrounded by the pelt of a lamb. He was stubborn, but as he best could be. And smart. Likely enough to best me were it to come. But nay, he would refuse.

And the serf, little Alium. What of her? She was ne'er to be mine as I wouldst sooner have a sword. Yet, she doth need protection and guidance. My friend Caducus, Sir Caducus, he'd best that for her. Yet he doth refuse on that account as well. Why? No doubt to teach me something. Something I doubtlessly need forthwith.

My challenges on this simple quest had brought much against myself and much to myself. Upon me right is that which would risk life and limb to protect and assist me. Upon me left, a young girl walked of none I knew about. Yet she has had time to be on hers more than twice and remained. And, of all that is troublesome, Longwise, who has refused a rider ever of his life save myself, now had allowed her upon him. I was inclined to do that which I had ne'er.

Sir Caducus rode upon Gallant. The newly christened prisoner rode upon a steed. As did the two with which had quarreled upon the once too many and the last. And I rode Longwise. 'Twas a few miles yet to Juxta Iter and Alium yet afoot.

I wretch me hand out and took her to ride at me breech. She complied, and we resumed our path upon the Arbitrium Highway unto Juxta Iter. Rather the extra weight upon Longwise to

be a burden, he seemed game. I felt, even, a need to hold him back
just so.

"If you really fulfill *the* royal law according to the Scripture,
"You shall love your neighbor as yourself," you do well;
but if you show partiality, you commit sin, and are convicted
by the law as transgressors."
James 2:8-9

Chapter 7
The Tale of Iggy & Ira

Of that which we'd traveled within since my parting of Ementior, nothing had been more astounding than Rubropontem. Mostly upon the fact that all within were red. I wonder that they did worship the ruby stone. 'Tis yet a mystery to me. I had a thought that a man who doth sell red paint should be blessed within the confines of that place. Of our current path, nonetheless, Juxta Iter was as unremarkable as Rubropontem was memorable.

'Twasn't as ugly place, simply as common as one could fancy. It sat within a small lea from the edge of the mountain. Not more than a dozen small buildings. We came from the north straight upon a column of buildings to either side. Within the village, the highway presented a choice of direction as it splintered about left and right. We would, no doubt, have to enquire as to which the Arbitrium continued.

I was quickly given the directions upon which house the local constable lodged. Our curry, the thief and his former confederates, were given great notice. Most notable they were. As though well known to the local burgess for naught good. Were they favored due to the said relationship? Nay, but their conditions brought about smiles.

A collective accumulation of suggestions came about on our way within the town from our prisoner. He blasted our idea of bringing him to Juxta Iter. "Such is a fool's errand, bringing me within that ville. You shall only have your own heads to pay."

"You believe us such stooges as to suppose this prattle upon now?" I asked the knave clod. "After you have forced it upon our ears for this last five or more miles? And I would postulate that you would have us to what? Set thou free upon the country to recommence your havoc? Nay, we are not the fools such as you assume."

"Were I such that would wager – of a certain we neither are..." Caducus explained, nodding a smirk at myself. "Were I, the constable is not of family to this mongrel, and, indeed, seeketh his life."

With much stares and smiles, we were given the way to the constable's own billet. He stood without his door at our approach and stepped lazy into the dirt street upon our path. "Clepta Saccularius. 'Tis been a fast of days." He looked upon myself and Caducus. "'Twas a day, his own mother spoke of, he'd cross the wrong sword. A knight and yet one more." He looked at the thief. "None more for thee, you shan't come from this one, ye old cutpurse."

"I am Miratus of Ementior. My fellow knight, Caducus." I pointed at the two cross horseback. "His cohorts fared less."

"Please, come down. At the least, a meal for thee each." We did as he asked and dismounted our steeds. "I am Constable Preceptum. Welcome to Juxta Iter." He shook mine and Caducus' hands. Upon inspection, he disclosed the others. "Trica and Dolor. Confreres to that one. Me own blood. But from where, who knows?"

"'Tis true, then? He spoke of you as his cousin. In that you wouldst treat him special." We all looked upon the larcener. Of which he dismissed our stares, choosing the ground rather to gaze upon.

"Aye. And yes, he shall be treated special, indeed. Likely from the gallows before nightfall." So he said of his blood.

We pulled Clepta from his mount and assisted the constable to bring him to a steel barred cage within his garrison. "'Tis no reward for them, but you may search them and all you find you may take as you wish. Their steeds as well." He denoted the thief. "As for him, he shall need nothing where he is bound."

"This defalcator then, he doth have a train of wrongs?" Caducus enquired.

Preceptum smiled, deprecatingly. "Aye, he does. As long as me arm. And such for a firkin of years." He looked back into the cell which held the hooligan. "Since we ran the streets as loose and wild young boys. He found he could bully and thief upon people. A genuine ne'er-do-well. He wast and always will be. Worst of it upon this previous fall when the three set upon a farm house. Thought it to be empty and a peasant and his wife were slain as they were about it."

"Might I have a moment with him? Alone?" Caducus asked.

"As you wish. Do remaineth without the cage." The constable advised.

"Of course, dear soldier." Caducus left us as the constable led myself into an adjoining room.

He sat me down and called to his wife to prepare food. "I shall tend to your steeds and the deceased. And your serf, I shall have her round the back." He left the room upon his mission; and I sat, quiet and timid, looking about at the drawings and paintings.

Moments later, Caducus joined myself. "'Twas an interesting facet, you wanting to speak with that daft thief." I spoke.

"Yes. I concerned myself with his...heart, as it were."

"Ahh, indeed. Yet if such a one deserved no comfort within the life hitherto, 'twould be that snake. His loss, the world's profit." I retorted my friend's attempt to save the soul of a fiend.

"Upon which we will, likely, not agree." He smiled as though I was still a child, still trying to grasp the values and considerations of life. A fool, he or I? I was certain it were not I.

"Preceptum is stowing ours and tending them. Alium should be about the back so she may eat." I said, indifferently. "I suspect we can use that which we gain from their possessions."

"Indeed. At least a ride for dear Alium. Mayhaps to sell the others and gain a few pence." He said. Still within an uncertainty I agreed. The horses could fetch 15 to 20 pence each. 'Twas a sacrifice to keep the one for young Alium. Yet I would not have to have her ride with me.

"I ponder her presence. We should sell her here, within Juxta-"

"You fool! She is as you and I. You cannot sell her. What monster might have at her by way of a few pence?" Caducus rose his speak to ensure he was heard.

A moment allowed my anger that had risen like a gale in seconds, to sequester a bit before I spoke to the matter. "My dear Caducus, you have been asleep this whole time? No matter your thoughts, your ways. None upon the plans and wherewithal of that lush Albus Civitatus of your own, here 'tis a serf. A slave. She is property and is treated as such." He quieted a bit.

"Aye." He replied at length and solemnly. "Yet I will not agree to any that involves her as such. She is but a child to me and that is the best and least I shall consider her."

"Very well. I shall concede your opinion on it. 'Tisn't accepted hereabouts. But I shall honor yours by not selling her." Within me I fought to acquiesce. His opinion, valid or nay, I had me own world to contend with. "And the horses we now have added to our herd?"

He thought but a second. As though he'd already planned. And, as he is, this I know, he had. "We sell two and keep the prime for Alium. Unless you doth enjoy the crowded saddle upon Longwise."

Alium was my property. Not the choice with which I made, but as it fell upon us all. True my life might ne'er effect that without the land that I trudged. The adjudications and accords that are made at my hand will ne'er vacate the Urbe Mortuos unto life, yet I had say upon a few lives within me own grasp. Alium, somewhat Caducus, and that of mine ownself. 'Twas a chance to do good? Or a chance to be a fool? Fool or not, I desired me own saddle. "Yes, we shall retain one of the beasts upon which for her to ride."

Yet sale of the beasts proved difficult. 'Twas a poor region. "I can tender a paltry sum. Appears you've little choice." The constable offered.

"Nothing short of what has been upon the table. What dost thou offer?" I asked.

"'Tis all I can. Ten pence upon each. Nary a bit less, but I shall try to re-sale them and pay you the difference if thou comest back." He offered up.

Caducus looked upon me and nodded. "That will do. That and the vittles you stowed for us and the savory meal your wife made. 'Tis enough." I handed the horses off to his hand, and we mounted our rides. He tied them hence and disappeared within the billet. He returned a moment later and handed up a satchel of silver rattles. I took it and stashed it away.

"My thanks to you for the ceasing of this cast of rabble. Their trouble shan't be missed upon Juxta Iter. Nor upon the region." The constable said.

"Was a thing we welcomed. Though a bit discomfiting upon the highway." I looked at Caducus and Alium. They both appeared ready. Then back at Preceptum. "My best, sir. Gracious blessing and good day." The constable bowed, and we turned our steeds to the west as he'd enlightened us with which to proceed. The way would turn south again in three and less furlongs as he'd explained.

Our cursory gait took us to without the small borough within minutes. Though we had spoken to none, the townsfolk waved and were albeit friendly. As we left the buildings behind, I looked upon the young serf. "She is a fine mare that you fancied. Yet, I would have chosen the bay. He was sturdy." She smiled, clearly well with her own appraisal.

"M'lord, she is a fine animal. 'Tis a gracious thing that you do." She bowed to me from her saddle. "I shall care for her lovingly so long as I am upon her."

Caducus' apprehension was better of me. "'Tis yours to keep." Her words were of one that was to borrow. The cognition of it did not come upon myself. But, of course, a serf were not allowed to own such a thing.

"M'lord?" She looked to me. She knew this as Caducus did not.

As to the owner of the horse, I did not consider. I pulled the leather sack of coin from my satchel. Was not upon me that we bested the highwaymen. "Half this be yours, my friend. And half the horse, I suppose."

"Nay, but she did her part. The breed be hers." Caducus insisted.

"M'lord, I cannot. 'Tis not my station." She said to the other knight. He was openly sullen of this. Though he did not speak. I believe that he was within an advent to accepting. Of being aligned, no. Yet seeing a change of that which irked him so much was not to his grasp.

He was not to give in at that, yet. "Very well." He pointed to the tiny leather poke in my hand. "You retain the pence." He then pointed at the mare that Alium rode. "The horse is mine."

I saw his intent. "So be it, my friend. Yet, assuredly, your heart is grand; but your head is unshakable and cussed."

"Naught, dear Miratus." He proffered his hand palm up towards the girl. "Hear this. The animal is mine. Yet I cannot maintain two of such. I shall need one to oversee her and tend to her. And, since upon two I cannot ride, the beauty is your burden. To all that is needed of her. 'Tis mine only in name."

"A great strategy, Sir Knight." I said. "You have a bit of genius within that promontory of yours." A moment late and I was aghast suddenly that I agreed to such that would circumvent the ways and laws regarding a serf. Yet, I recalled again, that which she had done of which did keep my soul within the purviews of meself. And thus, I let it to be as it was suggested by Caducus. *Ita fiat, esto.* So be it.

By the hour we had agreed upon the method of charter for the equine, we had made the few furlongs and the Arbitrium had turned south again. "M'lord, I do remember this route. We are indeed pointed to Inlitora. 'Tis a fortnight off." Her eyes darted about. She concerned herself to be chatter out of turn. Neither of us commented or hushed her. "Through the Eremus we shall journey."

I pulled the skin from my satchel. "Eremus? The desert? It is not upon my way. My map." I pointed out.

"Nay, m'lord, but it is there. A day within it or more we shall be." She replied.

"How long ere?" Caducus asked.

"Mayhaps, two days and we should be upon her. But I am dubious for the proper time. Could be more or less, yet 'tis close." She nodded.

"It is good we know. We shall keep our flagons filled and at the ready." I added.

We ambled a bit more and Caducus spoke. "Trica." He said to Alium. "He was the owner of that mare, was he not?"

"Yes, m'lord. It was he." She cocked her head. "Be it that he was slung to her, that is." She patted the mare's nape.

"I do not recall any mention of the beasts' name. Dost you have one?" He asked her.

"'Tis your horse, me lord." I was certain, as did she, he would lend that honor upon her.

"'Tis true, lass. Perhaps you would have a charge?" He offered her.

"Aye, m'lord." She said.

"Well then, child. Let us have at it!" I demanded.

"As you wish, m'lord." She swallowed within and smiled. "Libertas."

I fought again within me, for I knew the source of such a name. Libertas. Freedom. She could not have her own freedom, therefore she was to name a horse, all but given her, by that moniker.

As was such for Caducus, he found a laugh within it. I fought an anger down. A storm within my chest. 'Twas me right, but I weighed the need. She was honorable towards myself. I had in me to demand her otherwise, yet I would not because of her mind to me. As such, I felt, she deserved this to her. I battled and conflicted the one or t'other inside. And then, twice upon a single day, "*Ita fiat, esto.* So be it." We rode on.

◆ ◆ ◆

The Arbitrium Highway continued. As it had been off and on from south of Rubropontem, it lingered near a river. A waterway of which I had no name. Of a certain, it had one, yet I knew it not. I grasped that knowing the imminent desert would give us precedence to be ready. To be prepared for the draught we'd experience.

"Alium, wouldst you know that distance to Eremus now?" Caducus asked.

She looked at me, seeking permission to speak I presumed. I nodded. She looked back upon Caducus. "'Tis a bit. Three days, m'lord. Perhaps a bit more. Three of a certain."

"Shall the river remain with us that span?" I queried.

"M'lord, just a day's journey this side of. Yet an oasis is near half into the Eremus." She said to me.

"Well established?" Caducus asked.

"M'lord, indeed." She said, looking to him. "We had a bit there upon our passage to Urbe Mortuos. 'Tis the tenure of two brothers. One who is nice and t'other angry and mean."

"Aye. Then we shan't stay about it long." Caducus spoke for me. Yet I requested it not such.

"Indeed, there shan't be a point to do so." I agreed.

"They have a shop there. Of goods and needs." She added. Such she did little. T'was not a common thing for her.

We continued on. I watched upon the river fair. It was well and wide. With more banter, Alium produced that the estuary flowed unto the ocean near the manor of which she belonged. It diverged from our path before the desert and returned a day or so upon leaving Eremus.

Once again, we discovered a proper camp. Caducus and I hunted meat as Alium founded the bivouac. She sought the woods for herbs to cook the paltry grouse I had managed upon. Caducus returned empty-handed. Notwithstanding, Alium managed to make the creature such as kingly mutton.

Upon the morn I found seclusion and bathed within the river. Fresh and cold, yet such restorative. Soon we were back to the highway. Of such, wound and twisted. Much often little more than a trail. At times wide enough to rival the entrance to the king's palace.

I thought upon that. 'Twas as years ago. In truth, deficient some days of a month. Yet such remained upon me. Though 'twas me king and homeland, I found that much about me was more. So the distance made it such. It was that I was better, yet unhappy as such. As though to spit within the eye of that which I had been making it evil. Yet, how that could be, I was confounded. Yea, when I looked at the man Caducus, I found meself jealous. How it was that such a gentleman could best myself, yet not appear to attempt such? His was a different lot, for certain.

And young Alium. Hers had fallen to me. Of such I had no need or desire. She was but a child and a serf. Were it that Caducus, the noble, yet had taken her from me, t'would have been simple. Such still mystified me. He'd have, no doubt, set her upon her own. For the very thought of owning such a thing disturbed the knight. To his own instability, I believest. Yet, it would have been such a likelihood that he could have eased his own mind and given her true freedom. But he refused. Again, to teach me upon a truth he saw, no doubt.

Coterminous days proceeded likewise. Each I let me own mind talk upon myself more'n I should have, I s'pose. 'Tis nothing now, but I quarreled distressingly within. A charging would have done me well, yet we saw no one or no thing. The day the river wandered off, we dipped to cool ourselves, then re-filled our casks, and bid it ado. We determined to drink simply that which we were to need as the heat rose. The brush and leaves dispersed and were swallowed up by the grey and fire red of sand. The land about became barren and empty. In mere furlongs.

The heat grew quickly, and I found it odd that we drew nearer the great sea in said state. "Such a horrible land."

"'Tis a mere bit that we cross, m'lord. The heart of Eremus is far to the west. Lord Iggy said 'tis not crossable. None can carry enough water." Alium spoke to me wonderin's aloud, pointing with her hand.

"Who be lord Iggy?" Caducus asked. Such as was me own thought.

"He and his brother, Ira. They own the shop at the oasis." She bowed her head a bit. "My lord, forgive me. Their names are Ignavia and Iracundia."

"No need child. There be no offence." Caducus spoke for me. He doth get beneath one's hide.

The travel within the barren land was of such, I wished for home. Yet it was not as wearisome as to sleep within it. I suspected the heat to come down with nightfall. It did, but such that it was unnoticeable. And the dear sand, soft to rest upon, was on and within all we had and all we wore. Such it was everywhere.

'Twas upon the second day in Eremus I readied to lose me mind, and we saw the oasis. That which lasted a moment and it reappeared at a greater distance. I kept my vision upon myself. It yet happened again. And, yes, once more. We were destined, nonetheless, for a single more night upon the sands first.

As another day edged upon us, it was such that I realized per chance, the pence that I had upon the value of the horses should have been spent for dried meats and fruits. A ferreting of game and catching thus, proved upon Caducus and myself a bit to challenge the wherewithal of. Even at once a day. The game did not prefer the desert any more than we. Alium's mention of the shop encouraged us. Water enough for that distance, yet.

It was then, near past the apex of the sun, that we did see the same oasis. Which upon, caused a bit of a celebration. 'Twas an hour off as we saw from a rise of sorts. But we did concur it was real.

Upon our approach I saw it was not unlike any other shop. Yet for the locale, within Eremus, it would not be of much note. An edifice of non-descript. Of poorly milled wood, and a good size. My chimera idea had that of a large well and water about the place. Trees, shade, greenery. Yet stood a few trees to the post of the building itself, but not about the highway. The well, that itself was not to be seen. "Where from does one get the water, dear Alium?" I asked.

"'Tis within, m'lord. Closely guarded."

"They nick you for it?" I asked.

She felt the anger rise in me. "My lord. Yes. 'Tis an expense."

I considered the water we had yet with us. Was not enough to bring about the other end of Eremus. Had I purchased greater canteens in Juxta Iter, filled from the river, we could avoid the thievery. But it was that I had the pence. Pray that it was not beyond that I could pay. I worried greatest of the horses' welfare. They required larger amounts than that of ourselves. Indeed, they were the chief consumers to now. We came upon the building and dismounted the steeds. "We shall see the cost of this visit. This oasis." I said.

No stables about, we wrapped the horses' reins upon the posts without the porch. I heard, nor saw, naught of any about the outside. "Hello?" I spoke towards the open door. "'Tis any here?"

"M'lord, yes." A young serf came to the door. He wore a dingy blouse and equally dingy leggings. It was once that they were white. Or closer thereof. "Please, come in. We are open."

The dingy color of the serf's clothing was that of the red desert sand. It was yet upon myself and that of me companions as well. By much greater upon this market steward, though. His was that which would not be gone with a wash. Caducus and I walked in. 'Twas a fair place with much wares and even a few trinkets. I was most interested of the dried meats, fruits and berries, perhaps. And water.

Within the center of the largest room sat an odd looking table. Round about with a very heavy looking wrought-iron top. It appeared to be of two pieces that pulled apart, yet were kept in place by a very sizeable lock. "And, young serf, what be this?" I ask, pointed upon the gangly contrivance.

"Dear me, my lord. That be the well. 'Tis the freshest water of all that is in this region." He spoke, excitedly.

"Ahh...likely the only here abouts." Caducus moaned abaft of myself, nearer the door. "Should be free to refill our casks. Not locked there as a prisoner."

"'Twas a time it ran dry. We are such careful of that now. We must live too." The slave said.

I looked upon the young serf. He was of 20 years or less. 'Twas a bit hard to say of a certain. "I cannot take thy word, knave. 'Tis not believeable. Sounds as something your master spoke to you to say unto us, the traveler." I looked at my companion. He frowned. It was that he frowned to my speech or the lie I was just told. Made no difference. We were of a need and the cost was as it would be. I looked again at the dark-skinned boy. "How much shall it cost us?"

"That, good knight, should be determined by me, not the slave." A large man, of which sat in a chair that moved about, came from a room posterior of the counter the serf stood breech of. "You show unto myself the casks. I will tell you how much they shall cost to fill."

'Twas an odd thing, this chair. As though his legs were not able to move about upon themselves and someone had affixed wheels to allow him such. The serf assisted him with a moving by pushing. It was that it seemed a great feat, too. The man, a horse in size, offered none to lighten the load. "Bring the casks, I shall tell you the costs." He repeated. I fear my thoughts were bound upon him. Was that I had ne'er seen a man of such girth. "Knight?"

"Yes, of course. Miratus." I stumbled upon my words. "That is, I am Sir Miratus, of the city of Ementior."

He was a bit sharp of the tongue. "Yes, I am Iggy. Of the Eremus." He did not smile. "Now get about thy needed casks, yet, or move on."

I turned to find that dear Alium had fetched them and brought them within at that moment. "Alium, dear child, thank you..."

"Out, child. The only serfs that come within are here to work." Another voice screeched upon me ears. A second man came from the same door. He looked enough as the other to ensure their brotherliness. He, opposed to the large one, was smaller, yet not frail. Near me own size. Yet, again, smaller. That in the wheeled chair was in simple garb, but he that which had just came about appeared ready to battle. He wore mail upon his body and a sword dangled from his right side. Such a shop keeper?

Dear Alium, frightened, charged the porch and Caducus, with a wayward glance upon the miscreant, followed upon her. He took the casks from her and came back. "'Tis a fair sum at 10 pence. Fill them, drink thy fill and re-fill them again." The man in the chair said as he looked upon them.

Indeed, I was aghast. I had gotten 10 pence for the beasts gained from those who had set upon us pre Juxta Iter. Clearly, these charlatans were no less the dagger-wielding hooligans as they. "'Tisn't fair. Indeed, 'tisn't close. A pence and none more, thou scoundrels." Caducus, seeing such as I did, stepped forth with foot and tongue.

So he was met by the one with the mouth and sword. "'Tis the price. If ye feel the need to kill or be maimed your own self, for the water, so bring your sword and a duel it shall be." The bore dribbled thus a challenge. Of which I had not the patience to endure. "Thus prove your frailties as a knight. Not to mention thy dishonor." Both stood at toes, hands upon their hilts, ready, Caducus and he.

"Your words are a might rough, yet they be true." Caducus backed away. It took him a moment alone to see none there in the shop was the value of either man's blood. Still the shop keep did not back away.

"Like as not, you thinkest your station a might higher than our own." He spoke, red faced. "Bring forth the now 15 pence for your water, or be gone."

"You knave. Truly, thou hast lost your faculties." I said unto him, now stepping forward. "You doth play upon a knight's needs for gain. The water is not thine. 'Tis water, you fool. Not a trinket." He had not lowered his sword. And he did hold it as one who had used such more than once.

"Thy name calling shan't change this footing." He lowered his sword upon the ground. "Word to be those about, two knights fell upon shop keepers and murdered them for the sake of their water. I cannot believe thou would want such a thing the world to know you have done."

The idea would be such. "Very well. We can come to an accord. But the pay cannot be so much. We have but just a small bag of pence with which to live upon." The man's serf had, until this moment, hid behind the counter. He stood to speak secretly into the angry man's ear.

"I see you have a serf. Your own slave? A knight?" He asked.

"Nay. She mostly travels as we do. We ferry her to her home." I knew that he would think us to be of more wealth were we to have a slave.

"Such would pay what you need and more. A simple trade." He supposed we trade Alium for a few casks of water.

"Such a fool would not live the time of myself. Her worth is not in question." I braced myself and fought to remain genteel.

His face turned red again. "I know that serf. She passed here within some weeks ago. Her master was leading her. She is his possession."

"'Twas a fact. We see her home as he is passed." Caducus said.

"Nay, but you have had upon him. You took her." The man belted out.

"Ira, do not rile them further." The man in the chair spoke.

"SILENCE, knave brother. 'Tis that I shall avenge the lord murdered of these two." He rose his sword again.

I had my sword in me hand a second upon this fool's fray. "This be your foolish engagement. Your ability mayhaps be great, but against two versed knights." I backed upon the door and Caducus, sword once again in his hand, moved to be on me right flank. A breath into this and a scream came from out the door. The sound of Alium. I looked to Caducus and nodded. He left the room and out the front. Looking to the two who were still there affront of my sworded hand. "'Tis something I do not see here. Thou hast a plan that will be dealt with."

"Brother, this should not be. It is not to be done." The one who sat upon the wheeled chair said, his voice rising as he spoke it.

"'Twill work as I want." He pulled his sword to his face and dropped it upon the floor, following it in a bow. I looked back at the other brother. An acquiescence. In such a term it confused me. A moment into it, something of great weight and speed fell upon me. Upon the bash of me head. Cursed for not wearing the blasted helmet. All went dark and, that I remember last, my face against the rough-hewn floor.

◆　◆　◆

The light that peeked within the room was such that I could barely see that around me. It was not much. Yet, for the pain in my head, I was thankful for the benign light. "How is your pate, my friend?" A voice came to me. Caducus. I could not see him, but he was there somewhere.

"Hurts as the sun burns. Powerful and constant." I looked about. 'Twas a dungeon of some kind. Small. The one bit of light that was there came upon us from a small hole within the wall, very high up. I felt a fool to have been set upon as such.

"Alium's cry came from the north of the shop. I was attacked as I came about the side of the building. Two grown men. I believe them to have been slaves." I could hear him shuffle off upon my left. And chains. He was in chains. I moved me own arms to find I, too, was in irons.

"We are shackled." I spoke to that which he was already clear of. "'Tis king or a criminal that have their own dungeon and shackles." Caducus mumbled a garish agreement. "Why?"

"'Tis unknown to me." He breathed deeply in the silence of that dreadful place. "Alium was being drug on to a back door of sorts when they leapt upon myself. She fought. I fear for her welfare now."

"I fear for our own, as well." I retorted.

I learned the goings on without us later. But for that time, we sat in sand and dirt. The brigands had taken my wherewithal. No boots, no tunic. None but my undershirt and britches. "I feel as though naked."

"Indeed." Caducus spoke. "'Twas the boots I fought for. Once we escape upon that hot sand, we shall need them most." His thought already of escape. I yet wanted to assess that which we were within.

"Have ye tried to stand?" I asked upon him.

"Yes. 'Tis possible, yet the shackles are banded within the wall low. I had to stand bent." I searched about me backside to find them. They appeared well within the wall, naught that I could dislodge. Leaning greatly upon the wall there, I rigorously brought myself up. It was as Caducus said. I remained at a very strenuous angle. Of which I could not withstand for long and sat back down.

My sight within the place had grown familiar. The figure of Caducus to my left was clear. To the far of the room I could see a door. It was near 20 or more handbreadths above the floor. So as to slow our escape, me mind answered.

Hours passed upon us. Caducus mumbled much. We were both thirsty. 'Twasn't a drop in that dungeon with which to drink. And none came to assist. Save us, the room, of which was oddly shaped (not a square, not a circle) lay bare and empty. As a cave, more than a room. The hole at the top of the wall had no bars upon it. 'Cept it be the size of me fist, it may have been a viable opportunity. Yet, the door be all our chance to leave the place. That twinkling source of light soon darkened and night fell.

"Must it be that er'e we go, trouble be about us?" Caducus asked.

"Indeed..." I grunted a laugh. "Such a simple quest, it were to be."

"Yes. It were." Caducus softly joined me in cachinnation.

"Fastus was, indeed, within our path. Then the girl in the Red House. She was...well not as she appeared." I chortled.

"Oh, no, my dear friend, she was exactly as she seemed." He laughed again. "Trouble."

"Haha...ahhh. Yes, that she were." I agreed.

"I recall of those I have met that fought many of their years to put away the things. Those which did greater harm upon them than would ameliorate them." He paused.

"And, I am curious, as you wished no doubt, what is it you speak of?" I begged.

"To wager. Some, a constant. To gamble off all that they have. And, indeed, to replay that over and over." He spoke of the time we visited the varius.

"Truly. Yet, 'tis ne'er been that a constant for me."

He looked at me, a simperish grin upon his face. As best I could see. "Certainly not now."

Laughter came upon us such that we both fell to our sides upon the dirt and sand. A moment of which and I could smell the ground well that we sat on. It stank desperately of that which comes of life. Feces and urine. "Uuuuggg..." I cried, forcing myself up again. "The rank...oh my."

Caducus had smelled it as well. "We are not the first herein." He breathed deeply, gaining a gasp of clearer air in his chest.

He and I spoke into the night. He told me of his King. It was a time that we had not yet talked. At least not too much of. Though, indeed, we had spent days now in travel and time together, erecting a true credence betwixt us, yet 'til then, we had not learned much of the other.

"Should He, then, come to rescue us?" I asked. "If He is this monarch you describe."

Caducus sat quiet. Then, as if spurned by great understanding, he ventured. "I have not the perfect answer to such a question. Doth you expect yours? 'Tis a fact that no King is like mine. I cherish Him as I cherish nothing else in the world, my friend. Yet, as any adventures through the lands of our existence, I cannot wait in hopes One might come to pull me from the midst of terror. Yet I remain faithful as He has oh so many years.

"My King is not like any I have heard tell of. Indeed, He is much different than all." I could hear his breath as though he smiled. I saw such a thing in my mind's eye. There was indeed a goodness about him I envied.

"Pray tell how so?" I asked.

He breathed that same smile. "I was readied to leave. He came unto me. Indeed, He encouraged me. He told me He would ne'er not be upon my right or left."

"I know you as good and as a warrior, yet I fear I may thee as a liar as well." I postulated to him.

"A liar?" His breath changed. I do wish that I may have been able to see his face. He did not anger, but was not pleased either. "How do you thinkest such a thing suddenly?"

"Do not take it so harsh. But to proclaim that your King, upon so many a duty, came unto you, upon your own person, to bid you off? Such is more than I am to believe." I declared.

He remained solemn a moment, contemplating how to respond, I supposed. I heard the breathing smile again. "True, that is as you would see. I do not wish ill upon you, but you have not had a King as I have. Yes, He finds a way to be with each of us."

"Such sounds so much fantastic, 'tis hard to believe." I resigned that I would not fight on such a thing. I was tired. "So be it. I grant that I do not know your King, and so I do not know what He is capable of."

"If you ever wonder at my own goodness, know it is He that is responsible. If you ever wonder at my lack, 'tis me." He replied.

Such a resounding account that he spoke of. "I should like to meet such a Man." I breathed that smile. "'Twas ne'er that I have encountered such that would grant the responsibility of his own qualities to the likes of another." I grinned in the darkness. "Should we be freed of this great hole in the ground."

"We shall." He reassured me.

I cannot recall that which allowed me to finally rest and sleep. Within my head I retained the fact that the floor was of such a stench that I would not lay upon it. 'Twas enough that I sat upon it. Several times my body wished to lay rather than sit up. But I fought. Even with sleep upon me, I ne'er fell.

The light that came through the hole near the ceiling was faint the next morn. Likely, as how bright it was the evening before, that wall faced the west. Where the sun doth set. I found that to be important. Yet, upon me own breath, I had not a reason that it was such. I found myself watching it become brighter and worried for Longwise. And, such surprised myself, the welfare of young Alium. Of which, I was not the only one.

"Dost thou worry of her?" Caducus spoke in the still, very dark room. His perception paramount.

"I suppose. Yet, I know not why." I replied.

"I do, my friend. I do." He assured me.

Thirst was present in us both. And hunger. Yet not as the thirst.

It became well into the day as we could feel heat coming from the small window. We'd struggled to our feet to keep our legs active. Else they stiffened and became sore. But for to lay long ways in the filth of the dirt, we were unable to fully stretch. It was that to move about only.

As we sat, closer to midday, from across the room, the door creaked and slowly opened. Caducus, nor myself, responded. That which was upon the other side of the door was dark, and we were not with the ability to see any movement or figure. At length, a slight stirring was made. "Shhhh..." 'Twas Alium. "I will return in a moment, m'lords." She tossed something at us. It was small and landed upon me right foot. I reached for it and realized it was a key. I looked upon the door as it closed.

I quickly tried the key and, certainly, it released my shackles. A moment later, Caducus and myself were free, stretching and bending as we had not been able. We found that the door was too high up to get into. We searched, foolishly, for a ladder or step. In the dark, I realized there were none. "Shh..." Dear Caducus said. "She said she'd be right back." Of which, her moment spread into many.

Finally, the door creaked again; and it opened. Alium stood there with a short ladder in hand. She lowered it to us.

From behind her I heard a man's voice, yelling. "Aha! You worthless vamp, you. I shall have you join them!" We had but moments to counter what was to be a forceful attack by our captors.

"Caducus, catch her." I grabbed her by her blouse and pulled her inward to Caducus' waiting arms. The ladder had barely been placed when the one of whom referred the moniker of "Vamp" onto the girl, arrived. Rather than to fight him, I stood upon the lowermost rung of the ladder, presenting the bottom of the door at my chest. I reached instantly out in the near dark, grasping for a leg, I prayed. I found his ankle, grabbing and yanking as the very world depended upon it. The abject cad fell with a robust thud as his head met upon the floor about him.

"Come, let us go." I said. The other two joined myself as we rode the ladder up and onto the floor.

Young Alium, that which among us being the only one
having skirted the building, led us over the fallen man, and on into
the remainder of it all. "Should there be others who suspect our
freedom?" I asked the girl.

"Nay. Per chance he was not heard." She said. 'Twas our
esteemed luck, he was. As we came within a long hall the sun had
lit, another man I had yet to have seen, charged us. He was slight
but, indeed, game. Having no weapons with which to dispatch the
mortal, I sidestepped Alium and swung with my right. Then my left.
Then he was done.

The building that we found ourselves within was not the
shop. It was off breech of it. I did not find it such until we egressed
the thing to the south. Another edifice stood there. Stables. Within
we found Longwise, Gallant, Libertas, and that which was our
wherewithal. Alium had gathered it and left it ready for us. Our
boots, swords, and all. We quickly clothed ourselves and mounted
our steeds. As we turned to exit the stables, Ira stood with those
we'd taken down in the house. They were each armed as expected.

"'Tis a terrible mistake you have made." Caducus spoke.
"Be gone and it shall not become paramount."

"Paramount?" Ira asked.

"Indeed, you fool." I spoke up, bridling and holding
Longwise from attempting to run them over. "Be on with you or it
shall be a bloodbath." I looked at Ira. "Your blood."

He stood there with the two; and I saw a ways off breech of
the shop, two more on the way. All dark-skinned, male serfs. I was
suddenly very sympathetic of their plight. "So, you have a man who
owns you? Blood and flesh? He shall lead you into battle with two

knights. We..." I bespoke Caducus and myself, so motioning with my hand. "Have faced much more together than any thee could thrust upon us. Thy blood will mix with thy master's." I nodded. "Of such, you are forewarned."

"They do not speak for themselves." Ira noticed the two joining them. He alone had a sword. The serfs had staffs or farming tools. "I shall offer you one thing. If thou acquiesces, you may proceed. If, perchance, you foolishly resist, then your blood be upon you." He pointed to Alium. "Leave her. Take ye the water thou needest and go your way."

I dismounted Longwise and led him back to where Libertas stood with Alium upon her. Caducus followed suit. I stroked the forehead of Longwise. "Take care of these two, old man." I spoke of Alium and Libertas and turned me back upon him. I drew my sword, facing Ira and his serfs. A moment later Caducus stood at my side.

"'Tis a bit from the Bravio, my friend. Yet these look a might easier than Lacertus and the hounds of hell." He said to me.

"Careful, 'tis men we face." I admonished him.

"Yea, the life of which the greater value. We'll have no jaw splitting here." Caducus said. I do believe he was serious, but smiled while he spoke.

"Indeed. They are smarter as well."

It is of such warfare that to cause a man to think beyond the confines of the war, he shall falter much more readily. "'Tis a final warning. You doth need a fair lesson, but not blood drawn."

"Shut up, fool. You need the lesson, not I." He spat upon us.

He drew near to circle, yet I wasted none, drove the lunge, and surprisingly, Ira was quick to parry. The largest of the serfs drove at Caducus. They were not stocky or fair of size. And one was far beyond the age of that whom should wield a weapon at all. Nonetheless, he did. And was thus, that which was removed first. Caducus, in his compassion, struck him with the pommel below his fist, bloodying his face and removing his sense of being. He remained upon the ground where on he descended.

Ira kept my feet upon the move. I looked for a way that he could survive. It was that the less affective his work were, the greater his anger grew. Of which took his skill from him. In but a shake, he would be dead. Yet I was that he should live.

A second serf charged upon me companion with great noise and angst. His weapon a hoe of some sort. Caducus slipped left and brought his sword up, breaking the wooden handle within two. He which had brandished it, backed away, fearful. And refused to return.

Of the two remaining, one had looked for a turn at myself. Busy as I was with his master, he now turned to Caducus. "You are losing your mates, dear Ira." He paused to look about. In that moment, I brought me sword hard about, knocking his sword from his hands. He backed from me fearfully. I pointed my sword to his heart. His anger had grown such that his face reddened as though the sun had had its way upon him. Which was such a great thing as he lived within the desert. He likely had lived red faced for years, if any as such.

"No, no. I beg you, no. Do not kill him. Please!" I heard from me heels. 'Twas the voice of his brother. I backed away and towards me left, edging Ira towards the right. This not only allowed me to remain with me sword between us, but I could see Iggy, his brother. As well, I was keen to move and retrieve Ira's sword. "Please, my lords, he is hot headed. And foolish. We both are." I looked to find the large man, not only without the shop, but standing upon his feet. He needed no help from the chair with wheels. As I had, the others ceased the fight, the young serfs moving off towards the back of the shop.

The old serf rose up, wiping blood from his mouth and nose. As yet the only bloodshed. Ira's anger still raged upon his face. "You cannot fight in such a state. 'Tis a sure death against such a good sword." Caducus spoke to him.

"Do not tell me how to fight. Perhaps you would give me the edge?" Ira returned. "Bring it to me, you frail fellow." His anger rose even greater. He had not a sword or so much as a stick within reach.

"You fool! The good knights have spared thee, worry them no more. We shall set them on their way before they truly wreak vengeance upon us and ours." The brother yelled.

"Listen unto him. There is no need to increase this." I declared to him. "This will be a foul end upon thee. Please."

His eyes wandered back from me unto his brother and yet to Caducus. He stood, arms reached about as though he'd prepared to wrestle now that his weapon had been seized.

"Fetch the fool forthwith. He has abandoned reason." The brother Iggy said to his slaves. The youngsters ran to Ira's side, tugging at him.

"Leave off, you culs. You will be flogged about for this." He resisted, still convulsing with outrage and exacerbation.

"'Tis your only chance. Should you return upon myself, I will take your life." I pointed to Caducus and Alium. "I will not risk the lives of the others in exchange. Heed your brother now."

At last, he relented enough to appear to be overcome by the serfs. The young men seemed more than enough to force it, yet gave their master lee to remain within subject of himself and the awful moment. He turned and walked jaggedly back to the rear of the shop.

As he receded within, the brother Iggy spoke. "'Twas a beastly idea to perform." He raised his hands to indicate the whole of the premises. "We have a problem we haven't the wherewithal to oppose. 'Tis a difficult time to preserve that which we have here. We must needs our serfs to do such. We have none to propagate it."

"Thou kidnaps the young girl to have more serfs?" Caducus asked, deducing the intent of the brothers via Iggy's explanation. His face near the color of the angry shop keeper moments before.

The man's head fell. He was shamed. "Yes, m'lord." He acquiesced, dishonorably.

"Thy keep is not deservedly yours. You both should be flogged of your very existence. Mayhaps twice and worse if I were to have a say." Caducus spouted. A serf was another person's, yet of equal in his eyes. Though he refused to grasp such was the life here, I admired the spunk he bore vehemently against that which he believed contrary.

"You speak truly, master Iggy. 'Twas, indeed, a beastly thing to do. Were we to tear the whole of your place down, 'twould be within the right of us for thy treatment." I added. "How should that teach thee good manners, however? None."

"Indeed." Iggy looked up at Alium. "'Twas upon her journey through to the north with her master that we garnered the idea. In palaver to the north, we saw that her master was alone. We spoke much of it and decided that were he as such upon his return, we should take the child. He would be rended and none would know him lost. She would be within the house, kept for babes. None would see.

"Yet her return with thou entangled the matter." He shook his head. "Still we had you. And the men were merry of the wife they'd have. Young though she be, yet old enough to bare and it was as though all was well. You would remain until you starved in the hole. Still, we had not foreseen her loyalty unto thee.

"A promise to be treated as a princess was not enough." He finished his discourse.

We pulled the steeds about and prepared to mount them, our swords still in hand. "'Tis a dead, dark day that your abode will be tread again. We shall tell all to the folk we see and the sheriffs of all establishments we pass. You should be fortunate that you live." I said as I reached Longwise's saddle. I throated my sword and clambered astride. Caducus did likewise as I settled in place.

"My lords, please." He approached us. I yanked my sword loose and swung it about, and he stopped. "Please, have mercy. My brother is a fool and..."

"Thy sibling should be locked away. He is a danger and an imbecile." I said.

"And eminently stirred." Caducus replied. "Is he as such always?"

The man cowered, telling us without a word that it was indeed a constant. He stood to full height. "My lords, I shall honor you and present you with all you need. Take from the shop as you require. All the water you needst and food."

"It is not that *we* need, but what of the next traveler? He shall need. Per chance he has a young female serf. Should you take her as well?" I asked.

The man, degraded in his manner, nodded his head. "'Tis the first that we have done any such a thing. And, indeed, it is greatly reprehensible." He rose his head. "Yet, 'tis only a serf. A slave. Of little consequence."

I raised my hand towards Caducus, as I knew he would advance his anger of what already was abundant. He yielded and remained sedate. "The child's welfare is, nonetheless, upon me own shoulders. By such treatment of her, you treat me. To which I would have none."

"You assume too much, shop keeper. Her value is of more to us than you would have. The next one may be the same." Caducus added, with temperament.

"Sir Caducus is true to such as this. Our value upon the child exceeds your own. And the next may be of the same thought." I agreed. "Indeed, we could have that of such that your lives were ours. None would fault us. Blood upon the sword of he who was kidnapped and held for death."

"If it please you, lords, yes. Our lives are in your hands." He agreed. "What wouldst thou have me do?"

"Yes." I thought upon it a moment. "'Tis a thing to guarantee."

He bowed his head again. "Upon all I have. Upon me own breath. If I should fail, your sword is welcomed upon my neck, m'lord." His hand rested a moment on the nape of his collar and then he looked back upon us.

"Very well, then. I ask only two things of you. To which is little considering your plans upon our lives." I held my sword to him. "First, that you withdraw the lock from your well. As a man needs water, so give it. Do not demand payment. Your establishment shall be the greater of it."

"Yes. Of course. Forthwith, m'lords." He bowed. "And that in addition?" He queried.

"Keep that mongrel from the shop. He shall be run through and suffer you all because of it. He has not the wherewithal to contain his temper." I pointed at the back door to which he'd been drug by the serfs as I spoke. "Find him else-wise to occupy himself."

"Aye, m'lord. He is truly a menace." He bowed again, backing towards the rear of the shop. "Now I shall fetch all that you require to continue your travel."

We made our way, once again, to the front of the establishment. I had Caducus remain on Gallant and young Alium upon Libertas while I retrieved our supplies. Upon entrance, Iggy had a bag of basics and a new, large cask of water. I had him fill those of our own. He meant to send us away at no expense. "Nay. We shall not be such. Our business is concluded with payment." He insisted the total cost was only five pence. I debated his honesty on the matter, being less than I took, but accepted his charges. Once paid and returned without, I mounted Longwise; and we were on our way. The steeds had each been watered in the stables. Indeed, much more value had been placed on them than ourselves.

Caducus drank nearly a whole cask full of water. We both suffered of great thirst. I drank much as well.

An hour passed into our travel silently. At length, I asked Alium how it all did go about. "Well, 'tis true they wanted to tend me as a princess. Such a room as I had ne'er thought to be within. I did not understand it.

"Novellus, the young man from within the store, he was gentle. I asked upon you both. He purposed that you were gone. I feared you had left. Worse, then. He inferred your death.

"I believed him not. That you were braver and stronger than such. He told me that you were *prope mortem*. Near dead. He seemed uncertain. They had to go about their chores. There is four. They had duties. I searched the house, as the doors were barred and locked upon from without. The door you were beyond was locked, but inside. I made to promise Novellus to be his. Were you two freed. He brought me the key." She smiled devious like.

"I sense a dishonest prose?" I asked.

"Indeed, m'lord." She looked down. "I do not lie easy. It was hard to speak not the truth.

"When he brought me the key, he said it was of the irons. For such I had to promise to wait until the lords were not present, or he'd be flogged. Mayhaps worse." She sipped from a cask. "The key of your room came from a small box. I paid it no mind. He was to watch me, but had a chore. I remembered the irons and searched the box. There was but one key besides that. It was to which opened the door. I prayed it to be the one and took it to give you."

That what remained in her story we knew. Yet I wondered. "Alium, speak of this room. Of their plans for thee."

She smiled, shyly. I believe she had spoken more since we'd encountered her than most of a year's time. "'Twas a beautiful place. Large as a room given to royalty. With a grand bed, covered about in pillows and shams. Beautiful drapery and valances. Colors as such I had ne'er seen."

"All that a girl could desire?" Caducus asked.

"Oh yes, m'lord. A mirror. A real mirror. And a closet with all the..." She looked up at me and stopped.

"They had planned this a time and then some." I said. Her face betrayed her of guilt. Ashamed that she had amused the thought of it being hers for a mere moment. I smiled. "You have nothing to worry on, child." Her smile returned.

It gave me much to think upon. A pleasant life were offered her, yet she was loyal to her master first. It was upon this that I saw the serf as more than an appointment or simple goods. Indeed, she had been better to me, a step shy of a stranger, than I her. At any point. There was much, indeed, to consider.

"Their thinking were justified that you had been lavished upon and forced into motherhood." Caducus said. "Such is that which a slave endures." He was still quite exasperated.

"Indeed." I agreed with my head down, my eyes upon the road, my thoughts about their business. I knew their eyes rested upon myself, but I remained stoic and refused to return the looks.

As vinegar to the teeth, and as smoke to the eyes, so is the sluggard to them that send him.
Proverbs 10:26

Be not hasty in thy spirit to be angry: for anger resteth in the bosom of fools.
Ecclesiastes 7:9

Chapter 8

Inlitora

Our arrival at the fair city of Inlitora was, as such we had expected, non-incidental. We found our way to the magistrate and stalled our beasts. Alium found a bench along the cobbled street and remained. As was her place as a serf. Such was a doubt of which I remained aloof. My cohort abode with her. He was aware of where we were, but she remained oblivious. She being a quiet sort and accustomed upon the knowledge of a serf, ne'er queried of it. It was her to know the city of Inlitora, yet why we tarried within was not patent to her. She was bright, much so for a serf, yet I wished her to be innocent of my doings as I tread a new path and were doing so warily.

The doorway upon the office had painted the *Regionem Cancellarii*. The Regional Chancellor. I was there to inquire upon the welfare of Alium's manor. She had insisted she was mine, yet I suspected that there had to be others with which I could bestow her. The door opened to a demure and unadorned appointment. One simple large escritoire and a single elder man to bear it. His hand scraped upon parchment and continued such upon my entry, as though I had not gained the entrée 'tall. After a summary moment, I grunted modestly.

He did not look to me. "I shall be with you momentarily, my good man." The moment lasted an interminable time. A settee and a single chair occupied the floor near, yet I remained upon my feet.

At length, his hand rested; and he rose his balding head to me. "A knight. But of course. A thousand pardons, sir. What is that I may assist you with?" He stood as he spoke, removing himself from behind the great desk. It was upon my notice that my garb often nurtured a guileless respect. Deficient of great awe or stooping, but sometimes of use.

"Dear sir, art thou the magistrate of these parts?" I enquired.

"Indeed. Chancellor, magistrate, *justitia et pax*, general laborer..." He chuckled at the thought. A genuine *Jack Ominium Artium*.

"Might you be able to offer myself furtherance concerning a serf of me own?" I asked earnestly.

"A knight that owns a slave? 'Tis not too common within this region. Which, where with I might only help in this quarter. If you or your serf is from another, I cannot." He looked behind me as though the serf were present. "My acquaintance exceeds the area well. I do not know you, thus I unlikely can help."

"'Tis true, I am not from here-bouts. I am Sir Miratus of the City of Ementior." I bowed slightly. "Yet that which I have as a serf is from Inlitora."

"Well, my friend, in that case, I can assist."

"Is there a fee to remove the serf cast from upon one?" I asked. I said such without pause. For had I paused, 'tis likely I would not have said it. My heart spoke afore my mind could interject.

What I asked had not yet been asked of the man. Or, yet, was such that he had years to recall the last. He was confounded as though a great winged beast had lighted upon his floor. "You wish to return it upon its own?"

"No. She was not born without slavery. She has always been such." I answered him. "That I am aware of." I added. His countenance appeared a light pale. Somewhat ill, it seemed. "Dear sir, doth you balance well? I fear you are sick."

"No. All is well." He sat down upon the front of his desk, pushing off that which sat there on. "My dear knight, 'tis a...well, an abnormal thing of which to ask. Or do, for that concern."

I grasped it, but pushed. "Aye, yet 'tis no doubt upon that which I refer."

"As you wish." He rose upon his feet and returned to the distant flank of the secretaire and sat. "And your name be Miratus." He looked upon myself. "I cannot recall that name to be of a hall or manor hereabouts."

"'Tis not, good sir. She was of the Opulentus Manor. Somewhere, here abouts." I construed.

He did not reply, yet turned even greater blanched in color. "My friend, knight or squire, you ask amiss. 'Tis a great manor and should likely overcome you. They are immense in strength of their very own soldiers. It is that I most vehemently exhort you to simply return her upon them. Likely, they shall accept her and whatever tale you wish to provide."

"You are ignorant to the tale of which you refer. She became mine upon several matters that are easily rendered. Her master, Opulentus himself, was set upon and murdered by a most vicious creature. A hound of hell, so I think. I was that which slayed the beast. Having just come from the sepulture of the only heir, her holding fell to me as the demise of the animal, that being the controller of her by the death of dear Opulentus at his hands, was because of myself." I rested upon that.

"Yes. I follow thee and, indeed, if this be true, she be yours." He declared.

I was not well with the accusation of that which I spoke might be untrue. "Dear man, I know your station, yet please, do not sound as if you accuse myself of *mendacium* perpetration! Every shard be the utter truth!"

He rose as if to remind me of that it to be his house, not me own. "Young sir! Dost thou accuse me of anything?"

I acquiesced. "Nay. That I only wouldst sooner fall upon and pierce me own with a demon sword than lie on this matter."

He resumed his chair. "Then we are in agreement that as best we can, this matter should be concluded with all due integrity." He pointed to the door. "Bring her, forthwith."

I did as he asked and found the youngling. As it was not a custom for a serf to enter any building through the first or front entry, she clearly had nerves upon her for such a thing. Still, she did as she was told. When she stood before the praetor, as was common, she was hooded and little of her face was seen. "Child, remove your hood." To which she glanced up to me and I nodded. She pulled the cowl back to reveal her head fully. The man's face turned another cast of white. Near all color gone upon him. "Alium." He spoke. He waved his hand. "Aye, go on."

I nodded at her to return without and looked back upon the old man as his face fell into his hands and down upon the top of the desk. "You know her. I gave not her name to your ears. How is this?"

He remained with his head in his hands. "'Tis an arduous tale, my friend." He rose to his feet and walked to a small side table, whereupon was a decanter and several cups. He filled one with the wine from the cruet, drank it as if it were life. He then filled the cup yet another time. Drank it as such. Then once more. Having not an offer to myself, he left the empty vessel and returned to the desk.

"Well, my friend, mayest you enlighten myself. And upon this not a moment later? Please?" I begged. The story clearly left the man ragged. "Lessen thy load, mayhaps?"

He sat down as though exhausted. "'Twill be something that will change the face of the whole of the coast. Aye, then work its way inland." He smiled. "And a sound thing it may be."

Having seen the repose that had fallen upon him, I pulled the one chair nearby over and sat upon it before him. "Please do, resolve my burdening curiosity." I begged again.

He smiled and began. "The good man, Opulentus, was, as it occurs, a close friend. 'Twasn't a day, seldom, that I did not have luncheon, or tea at the least, with him. He was of my confidence, and I of his. Not of which I should be able to verify any of this, yet as my standing, it shan't be questioned. And I was on the know of his son's passing and his trip to Urbe Mortuos.

"Opulentus' wife passed of a plague some 20 years back. She was a difficult woman, yet he was deeply in love with the wench. He doubted a new bride. But within his home there were many serfs. Women. He had his choice, but was a trusted owner. He daren't touched a one." He mused a moment. "Yet, there be this one. She was a beauty. Amabilia. Such a creature should ne'er be a serf.

"She adored dear Opulentus. And shared his grief all those years ago." He halted upon that a moment.

"I see the length and direction thou turnest. She is Alium's mum?" I said.

"Shhh...dear fellow, 'tis such that the whole of the neighborhood needn't now know." Not that I had screamed it about.

"And as such, she is a true heir to Opulentus?" I whispered.

Not seemingly possible, his face paled yet again. "Indeed." He gathered himself. "But not upon her cast. She cannot, as a slave."

"And thus, the great fear in your face of myself giving her such a freedom." I gathered as he nodded to my statement. "So a thing shall upstart and cause such a rolling across the coast it should cease the tides?"

"So said you rightly. Dost thou still wish to repeal her captivity?" He enquired of me. "You may not envision that which your fancy to do such a thing could, indeed, create. A most disturbing circumstance. The manor of such that I describe suddenly becoming under the holding of a serf could precipitate such a dilemma that the whole of this realm could be up-ended. Then on to greater and yet weightier disputes and botherations, as serfs and slaves from other manors and estates desire that which the Opulentus' pairings have. I am certain that as the youngster dear Alium is, she will likely, as not, set the whole of the manor free to live as they do please. And, times a year or more, or yet, then we should be mired within a war. At the utmost, possibly." He smiled. "'Tis such a thing, that which you consider."

I did consider this. As now, I did. Afore, it was to let a young girl free for she had earned such a thing from me. And whilst I cared not for the ownership of such, it was not to me own to tell another that he could not. Yet, I now saw her as something greater than a property to be bought, sold, or, indeed, used as an animal. During time as the property to any cast but their own, they were to be as the owner of such desired. To their very lives.

"Indeed, this journey has had its claws and pillows upon me." I took a deep breath. "Me mind doth tumble at the lessons and questions." I stood. "Pardon my exit, dear sir. I shall return post abyssal concerns and deliberations." I turned to leave the locale.

"'Tis best, for the time now, this not to be distributed as a handbill. Even the very thought shall disrupt the whole of Inlitora and our fair conurbation." He spouted as I opened his door.

I stopped and looked to him. "Yes, so I shall keep it within me own thoughts. As should you." He nodded an affirmation, and I left.

The street of cobble ran the east to west, in line with the shore. The great ocean was a thing I had yet to look upon. Caducus and Alium had found the bench they sat upon a bit to the west and upon the fair of the way. I chose to find a path betwixt the establishments and pursued the smell and noise of the sea. 'Twas a short traipse to the rocks that hung about over the shore. I wast not ready for the distraction of the mightiness of the water. For as far as I could gaze, 'twas all I saw. And heard. My heart beat the words that I had wasted many a year thinking of what the beauty and fearfulness of this were.

"'Tis an august and terrible thing to behold, is it not?" I heard a familiar voice upon me breech post some time within the lure of the ocean's beauty. I turned to see Caducus there. "Me thinks thou hast not come here just to see this, even so. You have much upon your face. There is trouble?"

"Nay." I replied. I looked back to the waves that plunged upon the black rocks below. It was indeed fearsome and terrible. The pounds of which I could feel in me chest.

"Of a truth, we have not been upon this path together long, yet I know there is more to what thou is contemplating than the ocean." Caducus spake to me.

I was not that quick to open my mouth to him as I had just upon moments before compacted to remain silent on the matter. Yet, still, the promise was not to broadcast it as upon a handbill. His sincerity and rectitude was as I felt trustworthy. He stood upon my right shoulder. "Your sagacity would, indeed, be of a treasure. Yet, I feel, on this, thou own desires might obtrude."

He remained, the trifling wind blew; and I looked to see him watch the waters. He was of a stoic moment that he wasn't attuned upon often. I returned my gaze to the waters that entranced him. A breathing passed, and he spoke again. "My candor is that which you wish? I cannot part that from who I am." He looked at myself. "'Tis of the fate of Alium, an easy perception. So, at all costs, set her free."

"Aye, it is..." I said. "And all costs could so well be such a thing." I turned about to face the village of Inlitora and raised my hands to encompass it all. "Such be the costs, perhaps. And perhaps much greater."

"A war?" He asked upon it.

"Quite possibly." He was far more insightful than I had perceived.

"How dost a war appear upon the horizon for the sake of one child set free?" He asked.

I looked at him. He was, indeed, the truest man I had known and that which I honorably called my good friend. He was naïve to just the point of genuine. Yet, a great man, a great knight. The truest of hearts. A sincere knight for that which a knight should be. "She is the only heir to the Opulentus Manor. One that appears great, if not the greatest of the region. The magistrate knew Opulentus as a close friend. Should she be freed..."

"Yes, I see it." He mused. He smiled.

"'Tis a great and serious thing, you smile. With humor, yet?"

"Do not read within that which is not as you think. I do see the severity of this." He folded his arms about himself. "All good is good. Yet not all good is without pain and suffering. What is right must yet always be pursued. The cost, therefore, accepted for the sake of the ensuing eventuality."

"Your argument, dear Caducus, though sound, does not offer solutions." I returned to my contemplation upon the deep brine. "She will begin such a fury, the world may ne'er be serene again. Possibly nothing as it is and possibly many – indeed, a great many - shall die through it. Much...indeed most, that of her own kind."

"'Tis the ongoing concern, my brother in arms. She has no "kind" of herself. She is as we are. The simple color upon her outside changes not who she is." He said.

I looked upon his stubbornness. "You doth desire to part the bristles upon me head." I grinned, looking back upon the salty sea. "Yes, I do know this now. Though my heart agreest, my head sayest you are the fool, you cannot change the casts of a thousand generations. Possibly more." I breathed the air fully within me.

"A simple quest I was set upon. Gain that which I was sent for. Destroy it. At best, return it. Then me name should be written within the annals of the kingdom. I would be a celebrated knight of the realm. 'Twas a simple task." I raised my hands again upon the ocean's expanse. "This, my friend, was not a part of it. Indeed, there is nothing simple of this task. Not t'all."

"Would it be that you annotate the difficulties with which could occur to Alium and trust her to not proceed as such?" Caducus required.

I looked upon him, somewhat of disgust. 'Twas not of his character, I so thought. "Indeed." I pointed upon the great waves below us. "And thereby, we shutteth the water tight?" I pointed upon the vague light of the sun, fighting to come through the thick and high murkiness of the fog. "Tellest yon light to stop shining that the heat should not become unbearable within the desert that we have just passed through days back? You, my friend, can be of such a dolt. One cannot explain to a slave that has known nothing yet that, thee are now unfettered and be thee quiet about it. She would laugh within your own visage."

His grin broadened as a river in a great storm. Wider, and yet wider. "You have seen that which is better and more than yourself, Miratus. Of a certain, you are not the man I came to know on the far side of the Rubropontem bridge."

"Death, sword play, danger and friends can have such a refinement of sorts upon one's heart and head." I smiled and placed my arm about his shoulders. "Though we be of different kingdoms, such is a truth that we are much alike. Brothers, indeed."

"'Tis an honor, my friend." He replied. We parted and for a bit, continued to watch the powerful sea. Its crash as some great explosion. As thunder, indeed. But he prodded. "And now, you have a great decision to decree. What sayest thou?"

It was within me. It had yet been such. Undeterred by that which may yet be upon the land, Alium was first the heir to that manor. And flesh as myself. "Yes, she shall go free." He slapped me upon my back and laughed out loud.

"I do know this be a solemn time and that many may suffer, yet 'tis a grand day that may well see the freedom of thousands before it has run it upon its full course." And so, he agreed.

◆　◆　◆

"My dearest knight, I can only say that this could be the beginning of a terrible time. The future upon Inlitora and this region may well be of a great catastrophe long upon us." The magistrate said. He was grave. He sat, again, upon the edge of the escritoire and looked at myself. I was yet alone as Caducus had rejoined Alium. He looked about the room and through the windows of the door, seeking another, I believed.

"What doth you look for?"

"My friend, I shall tell you of a secret that the departed Opulentus offered to me more than once." He leaned upon me, pointedly to me right ear. "He wished this very thing upon her. And some of the others within the manor."

"I am confounded. Why did he not?"

"Such as the same that you waited a time to choose. Fear of what may yet come upon this land." He smiled. "'Tis many in the city that wish the freedom of them, and it be banded upon man. No more. He refused, by and by, because he did live among us. He would suffer the consequences." He pointed to me. "Thou travels. You do this, then your feet leave. You return to that which you traversed, leaving thyself as but a mere legend or tale." He laughed out loud. "'Tis an amazing thing you decide upon!"

I smiled. Within me, my heart did beat. And hard, it did.

It was that little Alium had to fortify and settle questions that the magistrate had, through her, without her knowledge of the proceedings (though I do believe she was to be suspicious of it all). She was asked upon how that it was that I had come to be her master. Her recital was near mine that he agreed without challenge. Then, once again, she was sent to the bench to remain with Caducus.

"Now, my good knight, I shall write her papers." He sat upon his chair and retrieved parchment for the writ. He pulled a fresh quill and small bottle of ink from within the draw next and looked upon myself. "For upon the world, she will remain as a slave. Should she travel outside her manor, it is most important that the girl always have these upon her. It is that she will enjoy fitter clothing, yet still, many regard her promptly as a serf. Such an insult shall be reticent with this." He began the writing, then stopped. He smiled up at myself. "Dear fellow, this will take a part of the day. It shall be ready for the young citizen on the morrow. Sharpest of the morning." He smiled. "Hmpf...citizen sounds good upon her."

I bowed with the strongest of thanks and left. A moment and I met with Caducus and Alium. "Well, my dearest knight? How doth we proceed?" It was in me to hush him that I had nothing genuine to hand Alium at that hour.

"We needs to return upon the morrow. He said was something that would take the day to create and would be early morn." I said. My edging of the matter suggested to Caducus of a silence best held. He did.

"My lord, should we travel now to the old manor?" Alium asked.

"Indeed, let us be on our way." I agreed.

We found the horses and readied them. It was near an hour from the city that we found ourselves upon the Opulentus estate. It was a grand place. Fields of crops and land with great herds of cattle and goats. The road, well kept and even. Our path had wound east from Inlitora, and did slowly turn upon the coast. So that, as we came to view the manor itself, it stood upon the cliffs that did halt the ocean itself. Ementior had not the beauty upon such the most cloudless, bluest days. The manor was a consummate formation of perfect form and beauty. Such a contrast upon the land about it, yet set flawlessly within it. And great as a size that a palace may be. Opulentus was, indeed, a very wealthy man. And such was, upon that moment, that I came to see Alium as who she was: the mistress of such grandeur. Of which, to my shame, I held from her. I determined that I should expound. But how and when should I?

Upon our approach, a soldier rode out at a furlong from the manor and halted us. He was as though within a genuine army of the land. Owned upon by a king, even. He recognized my keep. "Alium?" He saw the owner of the manor was not present. "May I enquire as to our lord Opulentus?"

"Sir Miles." She said. "My lord Opulentus was struck by a beast upon the road. He is passed." As was this child, her words were few. With them came a horde of tears. I fear she had refused to gaze within the sorrow she held. As the lord magistrate had shown of the relations betwixt her and her master, he had, indeed, been as a father.

The soldier was saddened. He did not doubt her, but enquired after us. "'Tis an escort?" He asked. He was a freeman, it appeared. His skin was light, and Alium had addressed him a "sir." A knight, mayhaps?

"M'lord, Miles. I am Miratus of Ementior. My brother knight Caducus of the Albus Civitatus. We happened upon the child post the murder of your lord." I bowed within my saddle. "With greatest comfort for the loss of your master." Caducus remained silent, but bowed deep as I had.

The soldier, with grief upon him, nodded at us, knowing the presence required nothing of military needs. "Very well, then. Follow me upon the stables."

Lord Opulentus' stables were that which would garner a great man's awe. His was as that of a king. I oft marveled at his travel with a single child and not of these great soldiers he possessed. 'Twere he would likely be very much alive.

Upon the stalling of the beasts, we were thusly brought to the house of serfs that was near the capacity to that of the manor itself. Such prodigiousness. The grounds there about were hectic and full of enterprise. At our approach, I had seen many in the fields. The Opulentus Manor was, indeed, of greatness. From a distance, towards the fields, could be heard that of a voice calling to us. A moment of it and the voice could be understood to be that of a woman crying out Alium's name. 'Twas her mum, Amabilia. As the chancellor had mentioned. And a woman of refinement and beauty, she was indeed. Her dark skin gloried her features. She was uncommon of serf or freeman.

The two had their reunion, but I had much concerns about Alium. "M'lord, 'tis my mother, Amabilia." Her mother bowed deeply.

"M'lord." She acknowledged myself. It was that she knew not of anything that which had happened upon her lord of the manor as of yet. Holding the dear lady's hand, Alium professed all that had occurred within as curtailed of an account as she could muster. Dear Amabilia wept. As the magistrate had postulated, there were great feelings betwixt her and the master.

"And, of the beast, it was slain by my lord, Miratus. So therefore, I became his." She nodded and bowed in my direction.

Amabilia fought her tears back. "My lord." She curtsied. "'Tis a great thing." She looked at Alium. "So, therefore, of what shall we do? Seeing that lord and master to thou child, then went to bury his only?"

"Dear ladies, if I may?" I asked. They nodded in a slight bow, and I led them to a portico off the slave quarters. Caducus had remained with us. I looked at Alium. "Child, dost thou wonder as to my enquiries to the magistrate this morn as we breeched the city?"

"M'lord? Was to confirm you as me master?" She asked.

"Indeed. Yet there was more." I breathed a deep sigh and continued. "I was to locate the wherewithal of your freedom. I was askance upon that which it would do so." I suspected that she would be joyful. Her happiness did show, but not as I supposed it would. Such a thing tempered, I believed, by that which brought us to this end. That of her master's death. She remained silent, yet her mother fell upon the bench abaft her. It was that I believed she knew all that the account portended.

Alium sat next upon her, and the mother placed her hand on her leggings. "Child, 'tis of a something, that is."

I remained a moment as each did breathe and take the whole of what I said within them. Though I was not complete. "'Tis more, child. Alium?" She looked upon me. I smiled.

Amabilia rose her hand. "M'lord? May I?" She did indeed, grasp all that was a part of this.

I nodded. "Indeed, m'lady." I had not a plan to imply her ladyship, but it was befitting. Now, at least.

She did note the reverence and turned to the addled face of her daughter. "'Twas upon once that the master needed comfort. It was that I gave that comfort. He was as much my friend as my master. He ne'er forced himself upon even a one of us. He was gentle and good to us. Not a one wished ill upon m'lord." She looked to myself and to Caducus. Who, as the man he were, stood off from hearing.

"His is the greatest of honor and knows all. Lips that shall ne'er crack." I encouraged her.

A nod from the lady and she returned. "So, then, yes. Upon the loss of our mistress, he had no one. And I failed, due my compassion of him. I..."

This tale lagged, yet Alium was no fool child, being greater than her years. She saw this forthcoming. "He was my father?"

We both nodded our accordance. "My child, forgivest me. I did not tell you. He vowed upon all that was he wouldst tend you were I silent."

Alium remained stoic and silent upon this. She stood and walked back within the stables. Amabilia rose to follow. I put my hand upon her shoulder. "M'lady. Wait her out. She needs to talk upon Libertas. She is a grand listener."

Rather to pursue her myself, I nodded back at Caducus. He ambled after her.

"Now who be Libertas?" She asked.

"That which is as her. A beautiful, young mare. One she acquired, as it were, along our path." I looked back as Caducus entered the barn and sat upon the bench near Amabilia.

"There is much that I cannot do now. She will have her way."

"Dost thou grasp this? And to what extent?" I asked her.

The beautiful lady Amabilia looked at the barn then back to me. In such a proximity, I saw upon her the wrinkles I had missed. She was not the young woman I had first thought her. Still, the creases and furrows made her that much greater a beauty. 'Twas no wonder that lord Opulentus came to her as he had. Her smile alone could shift the greatest ocean currents just a repast beyond us.

"Wisdom bounds my tongue, m'lord. But I know she be the mere heir." She raised her arms to encompass the whole around about. "'Tis hers. Ev'ry bit upon the land. And beneath it."

I smiled. "Yes. Yet upon her freedom alone." She understood. "On the morrow, we shall return to the magistrate. He had much printing to do. Then, she will be set to her own life. He, himself will verify who she is and the manor shall be upon her." I looked at the dark eyes of Amabilia. A truly hard thing to pull oneself from. "She would need a guide, of sorts. One to lead her as she takes the manor."

Amabilia smiled through the tears that struck her face wet. "Indeed." She nodded. "I shall do what I can." She pointed to the manor and the fields. "There are many here who will be the guide. All shall wish upon her fruition."

We versed on. She doted much upon her daughter. A moment and she recalled the man who was her master and closest friend both. The tears returned. She told me of his life. Upon the falling away from his own father by reason of the way to which he treated the serfs. "He recalled once of the argument of his own insistence. He'd told the old man that treating us better would have us work harder." She laughed. "It was that he used such to lessen the foulness of his father. But it did truly become that way. We did indeed, work all the more. And that made his father an angry old man. He died such." She said.

From behind us I heard Caducus speak. "She is well. 'Tis all a bit much for her to understand, but only hurt some."

Amabilia and I rose. "Hurt? As to what?"

Caducus motioned us to withdraw. "She is troubled. To have known her father all her life, yet...to have ne'er met him as such. It is rending her a little. A moment and all will be fine."

I took the occasion to acquaint the two and explain the life that Amabilia had with the late Opulentus. "He appears to have been a good man." I knew Caducus would appreciate the past holder's treatment of the serfs.

Alium soon joined us. She had wet cheeks as to the tears shed, yet was better. I believed with her mother, they would, indeed, be able to tend the place. Though the future well could struggle with the many on the place that would be of her charge now.

◆ ◆ ◆

Morning found us, Caducus and myself, upon the road back into Inlitora. The day that lay ahead would be difficult. It was good that we had left dear Alium at the manor.

As the Chancellor's quarters came into our visage, it was a sight of confusion. No less than two dozen people gathered and fussed about. Mayhaps more than that. The reasoning of it all was lost upon us. 'Twas that they all seemed to want within at once. A mob, it was.

We stabled Longwise and Gallant a short block away and returned upon foot. I looked to my companion. "Yon *Cancellarii* 'tis a busy sort."

He smiled. "His bartering be quite a premium this morning."

"Indeed," I replied as we came upon the crushing mass gathered about his door. Of which remained closed and none seemed within save the magistrate himself.

One, that of a sailor standing, took upon us with disdain. "What ye be here abouts concerning?" He barked to us.

I have ne'er met a sailor. But he smelled of the salt of the sea and wore that of what I had seen such recited and sketched of. He sounded a might angry at myself, yet for which I had only to guess. I glanced at Caducus, who grinned having naught of a sailor himself, and looked back upon the man of the great ocean voyages. "'I do apologize, good man, but 'tis me own business." I genuinely wished nothing upon the fellow, yet he was game for something I did not foresee.

"Look here, 'tis one that has stirred this about." He belched out. I felt as much as smelled the rum upon his breath. I do not believe that he was in any way inebriated, yet such that he drank it that it remained within him.

"Now see here..." I spoke as he reached for my beggin's. A moment later, we found ourselves yanked forthwith to the confines of the magistrate's quarters and the slamming door latched behind us. He quickly pulled the curtains about and took us deeper into the front room. Nearly, as such, from view.

"Sit, good sirs. Sit." He commanded, pointing upon a pair of chairs within the turn of the office. We complied and were comfortably démodé of view.

"What is this of?" I asked, pointing to the mob without his front door.

He breathed deeply and sighed at the scene through his curtains. "Alium."

"How so?" Caducus demanded.

The chancellor looked back to us. "Nugae. That pitiless fool."

"Nugae?" I asked.

"Yes. Of a fortnight, he comes in the evening to clean and dust. He is truly a *gestor*. It is not within his capacities to see or hear a thing and not preach it about." He pointed to the papers upon his desk. "Last eve, he was here and saw the *forma libertas*. It took a moment's foolishness to spread the news." He pointed again to the horde about the porch. "Such an idiot am I."

"Yes, I see." I nodded. "'Twas a sailor, I dost believe, that was about to have at us." I looked upon the man. "What doth such have in this?"

"To the west of the city, there lies a great port. A number of ships berth there as their own port of call. Many trade in slaves." He breathed deep again. "They have much at stake."

Such caused even higher contemplation. Have I the right to create such a fervor? I pondered upon such a move. My dear Caducus, always the advocate of the lowly, perceived my doubts. "Such is the price of change, brother. You would give up what Alium has done accepted to alter the way now." He was right, of course. But he was not the one who would rile a few sailors. Then a few farmers. Then, even upon my compunctionous scruples, dare I say, a nation?

The grand chancellor that he was, reared to brave to consequences, sat within his leathered work chair. He smiled. I knew he was upon our straggled behalf. He would likely face reactions of his own community for this. Though he'd claimed to not be alone in such sentiments. "Well, my friend, shall we proceed?" He asked, willing.

I stood to my feet. "Indeed. Alium is to be free." Caducus stood beside myself, grinning as though he'd been the cat with the mouse that would have destroyed all foul rather than to have lit the fuse of such a thing.

The amused magistrate pointed at the *forma libertas*. "Sign, my dear sir, there." I did such as I was told. He pointed at Caducus. "'Tis a fortunate thing you came. A witness must be produced." He pointed upon the next line.

Taking a cue, Caducus signed where he was told. Some out the door seemed to have been able to see the procedures as the noise rose a pitch. The magistrate, brave soul he was, duly signed upon his line and quickly rolled it up. He slid it within a hard paper tube, sealed it and handed it to myself. "If she travels, especially alone, ensure she has this upon her person. Yet, though, with her status, she should ne'er travel alone. The times ahead may become quite dangerous to her."

"Yes. I shall explain such to her." I replied.

He looked out the window that was still exposed. "I thinkest I shall be without employment soon. Remind her that she should have a quality scribe and counselor on her payroll. I should be willing." He grinned.

"Indeed. An honest one such as thyself should be a welcome member of her household, I should think." Caducus enjoined.

With another short glance to the mob affront the building, he pointed to the back wall and the door that led within his own rooms. "Follow me. I dare believe thy life would be in danger. I shall lead you out the other way."

◆　◆　◆

'Twas early the morn two days hence that we rose to ready our continued journey. We'd spent a day to ensure all was well and safe. Much happened promptly post Alium's rise to mistress. She begged that we could stay on there. "'Tis been awful already. Many who are freemen have moved on. They will not serve a slave."

"Child, first call not yourself a slave hence. You are no longer such. And you will learn that those who do not support you, cannot be with you. When questions rise, those who will not ponder them and accept answers, cannot proceed with you." Caducus, ever the compassionate, held her close, comforting her. Had he remained on, I believe that he would have become every bit a new father to the girl. But we had that which we were destined upon before us yet.

Myself, had I remained, would have been as Opulentus himself. Amabilia was absolutely striking. Though I'd ne'er envisioned I'd have such a thought for a slave, I indeed imagined it now. But my duty had to be first in thought as well as action.

"I know the path you travel. To Insula Mortem." Alium said as we made our way to the road.

"How do you know such a thing?" I asked her. I had yet to even mention the Insula Mortem to Caducus. 'Twas the island of death, the bearings of the chalice.

"It is the destination of all knights that pass here. You are not the first." She smiled.

"You know this way? You know of the way there?" I asked her.

"Indeed." Her head drooped. "The great chalice. Many pass here to grasp the thing..." She grew quiet as I mounted Longwise. She suddenly grabbed upon my leggins'. "My lord, please. Do not pursue this. I have met many who seek the chalice. None returned. None."

I looked at Caducus. He appeared worried. More for her than for us. "Alium. We shall return. 'Twill be the first that has two knights come upon it at once. We shall have victory!"

She let me be. "Very well, but allow me to lead you to the trail that will guide you down?"

"That will be fine." Caducus said. She turned and ran to fetch Libertas.

"It shan't be fine, dear brother. I'd no intention of dragging this about." I said to Caducus, tertly-like.

He looked to me. "She has grown to us. 'Tis a chance we shall not have the victory you count upon. Such will give her a slower repose."

I did not like it, but it was done.

Within a few moments we were upon our way. Alium had come a bit and was much more willing to talk. And such, she did. She felt as a younger sister to myself. Of which I enjoyed. I took that time to talk about building up a cadre of loyal people. "Pay them well, train them hard. They will be loyal to you only. Treat them as you would desire yourself to be regarded." I had told her to hire the magistrate the day before, and she had agreed it was a good idea.

"Yes, m'lord." She said.

Caducus stopped Gallant, and we followed suit. "Dear lady. No man is lord to you henceforth. It is a thing you must curb and quickly. You must be stronger than all you discourse with. Ne'er believe them to be less than you, always respect them, but ne'er allow them to assume you are less than they." He said.

"Well said, knight." I spoke.

She looked to Caducus then at myself. Then back to Caducus. "As you say, knight. Such will do me well." She smiled. It was done right, yet at such a moment, it was comical; and we all stifled a hard laugh upon it.

Another several hours passed; and she brought us to a stop at a small, nearly unnoticeable trailhead that led off towards the now distant noise of the coast. "It is said an old man lives upon the trail. But none come from here that I have met."

We dismounted, and she insisted that it was proper to embrace a knight. She teared as we took our mounts by their reins and began our way, fighting the chest sobs our ownselves, upon foot down the gloomy, vague path. The fog did indeed make it much harder than need be; and in moments, our young lass was lost to the murk.

◆　◆　◆

'Twas another hour on the route that we neared the waters of the ocean. They ne'er failed to mesmerize my eyes and brain. The power of such like I had ne'er heard or seen.

Our solid path had turned to sand, and it began a much more arduous travel. We remained surrounded about by thick brush and shrub. I decided to be best ready for what lay ahead that I should ride Longwise rather than walk. Caducus agreed and did so as well. I led the way, but looked back upon him. "A quest, as by its best understanding, is that which a single does." I looked back to the trail before us. "'Tisn't that which is accomplished upon the backs and wits of a pair. Or more."

He remained quiet. Contemplating such a thing and the response that it needed best. But, finally, he replied upon myself. "I should think that you would welcome it. We have endured this journey, for near all of it, together. I should be amiss if I felt you were now upon your own."

"Indeed, you should. For we two are brothers now." I rode on a bit. "Yet now, this is a must to be upon me own for. As I do much thank you for all that you have done and been for myself, for Longwise. Indeed, for that sprite back there that now faces womanhood far too soon. Yet here, we part. If only for the sake of this journey upon the Island of Death, we shall rejoin upon my completion."

"And, mayhap you needst my sword?" He insisted.

I pulled Longwise to a stop and turned about in the saddle. "Then I shall yell very loudly." I said, smiling.

Below us the way wound again back and forth as we slowly moved both east and closer to the shore. A scant 50 cubits below us, next upon the path, stood a shanty of sorts. A small, nearly imperceptible column of smoke rose from it. "I should think the old hermit that Alium mentioned lives about." I said. We continued down the increasingly steeper sandy pathway.

"'Tisn't often I have visitors." We heard from the small, less than solid appearing shack. A man of such an age neither of us could clearly say, stepped from the hobble. He was bearded to his middle, grey and shaggy haired. His clothes (mostly a loose fitting robe of sorts) was a patchwork of colors, faded and stained. A patterned material was near imperceptible beyond the patches, dull as it was. He wore a rag upon his head as a worker in the sun would don. "You are on a quest for the chalice. It is a mere furlong farther down the path." He pointed towards the distant waters that now were loud enough to command our attention.

"You know the way much?" I asked.

"Indeed, there is a knight by here more than once a year to try their luck with Dentibus Igni, the guardian of the chalice." The old man giggled. "Please." He pointed to logs about the fire of which we'd seen the smoke rising. "Sit. I will make you something to eat."

It was upon myself to carry on, but I thought that I might gain some of that which I might need to retain the chalice. I nodded at Caducus, and we dismounted and found a bush to tie off the steeds. We sat that I might query the old man. Truth was that I had little to none of that which was really needed for my quest. The map was long minus detail. Caducus, upon either his ignorance or his rectitude, had yet to vigorously enquire as to my quest. The purpose of it all.

As the old man began his business of fetching and preparing said meal, I took in all that was about us. From the front of the old man's shelter, we had a clear view of the island. It was not readily viewable, yet the fog was lifting. I stood to look more closely. It was black stone and ugly. Small in size, it had but one feature. Devoid of all plant life, the only thing upon it, other than the rock, were a large keep of sorts. The remnant of a bygone castle with what appeared to be pieces of ramparts descending out from it. It was both demur and very intimidating. "Yes, the Insula Mortem. The home of the great Chalice of Tribute. Gold, lustrous, gem-encrusted, and most sought of." He laughed. "The quest of all the knights they have no time to deal with."

I looked back at him. "Pray tell, explain such a statement."

He laughed as he brought a hard, old biscuit to me. "Eat up, you will need it."

Caducus rose from the fire. "What do you intend with such a statement, old man."

"Haha...Timens. My name is Timens." He returned to the outside table upon which he was making something. I feared it was food. The place stunk of fish. "The quest of the chalice is one that they send knights to that they have no fear of losing." He paused and looked back at the island in the distance. "No one has ever returned from that place. No one." He grinned. "Thy opinion of thyself is great to have become convinced of success."

He looked at Caducus and frowned. "You do not belong." He returned to preparing his meal.

I looked at Caducus. "Explain thyself, Timens. What of my fellow knight says that he doesn't belong?"

He spoke without turning to face me. "You two, you are from different kingdoms, true?" We agreed. "You are here to quest the chalice." He paused and turned again to look at me. "Why is he here?"

"'Tisn't your concern." Caducus replied.

Timens looked at him. "You are right. It is not my concern." He faced his table once more and gathered food onto driftwood that served as plates. He turned back to us and served them up. Then added, "'Tis his concern." He pointed at me.

We held our "plates" and looked at him. "What upon him and this should I be concerned?" I asked.

"You, young fool. You came here upon a quest for something of substance. That fool chalice." He pointed at Caducus. "Why did he come? What is his quest?"

I felt foolish. It was a question I had ne'er truly asked. "I don't know. He has been at my side since he joined me. Faithful. Even saved my life."

"Foolish knight." He laughed and sat down. The insult would have garnered my anger a month before. Even of an old man. I looked down at my food. Which was less appetizing than muddy stones. I glanced at Caducus, who remained silent. "You are his quest." The old man continued. "He is here to gain you. To drag you back to his kingdom. It is his mandate to make you a citizen of his kingdom."

It was that our journey together did, indeed, fit the old man's description. I stood, looking now at my companion. "Is that true?"

He looked up at me. "Does it not concern you that this stranger proclaims this nonsense? His ramblings serve only to dismantle all that has been built between us brothers. We need to continue on." He sat the food down and stood up. He walked to Gallant and untied him from the bush.

"No. You go no farther." I demanded of him. "I go from here alone." I took the reins of Gallant from his hand and tied them back to the bush.

"Miratus. What are you doing? You know nothing of what lay ahead. I mean to be ready to help." I disregarded him and looked at the old man.

"You wish to convert him to your kingdom. Do you deny it?" Timens demanded of Caducus.

"I do not care." I said. It was no longer my focus. I was angry that Caducus had deceived me, but it all made sense now. I pointed at the island in the distance. "I only wish to know what is there. I will take the chalice alone."

The old man smiled and sat upon a log. I found a place opposite of him and sat as well. He pointed to the trail, which had wound around to face the west. "Continue upon the path. Ride your mount until you reach the water. Do not start with weary legs.

"At the end of the trail lies a small quay that is out into the water a bit. And a boat that is roped both upon the dock and the shore of Insula Mortem. Load into the boat and pull yourself across. 'Tis a hundred cubits. Not far.

"The keep of Dentibus Igni lies upon the north side of the island. The old castle." He pointed to the island. "You will cross the isle in the open. He sleeps or feeds during the day. You must be there in the day. And you must not wake him. In the dark, his senses becomes sharper." The old man enjoyed the tale.

I felt foolish again. I was not aware of the details. The old skin map showed the island, the way there. But that was it. "Who is Dentibus Igni?"

"Hahaha..." Timens laughed. "You come such ill-prepared, knight." He leaned across the fire. "The dragon of the keep. All fire and teeth. Black as coal and such a beast, the keep barely contains him." He leaned back up straight. "You cannot kill him. His scales resist the sharpest blade. You must take the chalice while he slumbers or not at all. And he has the scent of a thousand hounds. Remain down wind, else he shall smell you from the time you step upon Mortem, itself."

"And what shall keep him from coming after us?" Caducus asked.

Timens looked up at Caducus. "Only distance and time." He smiled. "He will not follow inland. He needs the ocean. He knows nothing else." He turned to enter his abode. "I have something you shall need." A moment later he returned with a drawstring sack. The material was garish and bright. And old. It matched that which he wore, but not as faded.

"What is this?" I asked.

"You shall need it to carry the chalice." He explained.

"Very well. Then I shall be on with it." I took the bag as I rose and went to Longwise.

"Brother..." Caducus said.

"Call me not such a thing. We are from different kingdoms, and it shall remain as such." I insisted. "You have led me as a bull by his snout and a brass ring. It shall be no more. Your plans had little to do save a notch in your enlistments upon your faith in your King." I took to Longwise's saddle, my eyes remaining upon Caducus. "Be thou upon your way afore my return." I wrestled Longwise a moment. "Else, you shall suffer it all when I do." I charged Longwise down the trail to the sea.

"The Spirit of the Lord is upon me, because he hath anointed me to preach the gospel to the poor; he hath sent me to heal the brokenhearted, to preach deliverance to the captives, and recovering of sight to the blind, to set at liberty them that are bruised," Luke 4:18

Chapter 9
The Chalice of Tribute

The path, sandy as it were, was not much more. It opened broadly upon the bustling ocean and ended before a small, wooden dock. On the other end the boat should have remained as Timens had said. Yet 'twas not. Instead, it floundered about betwixt the docks of here and there. I pulled Longwise up short and slid from him. The supports of the dock jutted up haphazardly, and I wrapped his reins about the one to my right. I stroked his forehead. "Should be simple and straight to it, old friend. While it remains daylight, the beast sleeps. I'll be back upon you presently. Then we'll be off to home and the glory of success!"

I looked about the place to find a course to which to gain the craft. Either storm or great wind must have brought it loose. The last upon this quest did not return, so it be that at least it was not tethered yon side. It's drift were not far, and I scattered about for a long pole or limb.

Having found none that would reach, I looked within the waters to gage the depth that I might simply walk it. Such was not too readily seen. The water was, yea, quite deep. Swimming with a mail and sword girded upon myself should, like as not, prove a fatal choice.

I glanced upon my steed and an idea struck. I pulled that which was upon him loose, the reins and all, tying them about each other, making a long rope of a sort. Upon the one end I fixed me sword and made a toss within the boat, hoping it would not land point down. Triumph was upon the first endeavor. I slowly pulled the bateau henceforth, and it was mine.

Of the speed my egress might need, I returned the reins and such to their place.

I ensured myself of what I needed. My sword secure, the knapsack hung from my shoulder. All was ready. I found my way to the boat. It was a scabby looking thing. But the bottom was dry. *A good sign*, I thought to meself. From the edge of the dock I looked upon the Insula Mortem. None had returned from thence. "Well, then." I said, barely hearing my own self above the crashing waves. "I shall be the first!"

The water betwixt the shore and the island was not as near rough of the seas farther out. The distance to Mortem not much beyond that which I could toss a rock. I prudently slid within the confines of the dingy, using the rope tied off to the far out dock support. There had been a small rope fixed to the gunwale for mooring. I had tossed it upon one of the pilings. I loosed it, then I began to pull the slack that was enclosed by the ancient metal eyes at both ends. Set to as a ferry at a common river crossing. Presently, the craft began to edge away. *'Twas a simple thing*, I told myself.

The island was nothing yet black shale. Alone, it was enough to make a brave man turn back. I was frightened from me own wig to the nethers. And to the nails upon my crusty toes. Of what, I could not yet say. But the thought of a bona fide dragon about my breech was not far from me.

The water was rough but not truly contrary. I made the small, twin dock upon the isle in yet scarce a few moments. I draped the same gunwale noose upon the opposite piling and balanced me way from the archaic skiff.

My feet upon ground, I took but a moment to be thankful. I checked and my sword and bag remained. Walking upon the loose shale was more than I had planned upon. I recalled that the beast was either sleeping or eating. And that he could smell me. The wind blew from east to west. I decided to remain to the west as I approached the keep. I worried more that he'd hear me as the shale kept me slipping and such made a horrendous sound. My worries were such but a moment, and I realized the noise of the boisterous waves made it burdensome to hear the clatter of the rock myself. "Should be about impossible for him to hear anything!" I spoke at the waves in the distance.

As sure footed as I could, I stumbled and lumbered about the western shore. The shale remained until the water itself. There were no relief of it. The distance to the keep seemed a brief stroll from the shore opposite. Now it was indeed a great feat to accomplish within the time I needed. Nightfall now seemed reasonable afore my capture of the chalice. I trudged on, fighting to remain upon the shore and not slip into the cold sea upon my flank.

A sudden misstep and, indeed, my wherewithal slid from beneath me. Having my sword in hand caused a loss of harmony and I floundered, doing what I could to retain it in me hand. In such allot, I slid, in contempt of it, all the course down to the water as it lapped mockingly upon the shale. One large boulder sat nearest me way, and I seized upon it. My grip brought me to a bold stop, standing me upright, flinging my sword forth from my hand and into the water. I had nary another weapon. I lunged to grasp it with me right, my left holding to the boulder. As I did such, I looked within the sea to find it and saw a horror of a sight.

There, just under the waves, lay what remained of a previous hero bent upon, no doubt, the chalice. He was mostly bones. His clothes near gone. Bits of sinew and what e'er it took to hold the ossein jointedly lingered enough that he appeared mostly about himself still. Empty eyes stared expectantly. His left arm strained upward to the boulder I hung upon. His hand seemed to have been lodged below what was such I could not move. Nor I and a few more, it was so broad. However the fellow came to be trapped as such, it was his undoing. My sword now lay within his rib cage. 'Twas an ugly thing for me to pull it from. Not difficult, yet grisly.

Post haste, I clambered back near the path I had been upon. I glanced to me breech and decided to climb higher. I surmised the boney lad below had fell victim someways as I near did, so as such, the farther I were from the salty water, the better. Up I went, slowly, carefully, and clumsily.

In time, I found myself near one of the old ramparts. What had been a wall meant to help retain the sanctuary of the keep above. Yet, even a castle at some distant time in the past. I carefully pulled myself to the stone that made up the rampart. Upon the other side of it a vast, wide hole had burrowed of rain and great waves. It stunk of dead fish and old mud. Its width demanded I to cross it. I did so, as carefully as I could. Yet the mud within was as slick as butter upon a roasting hearth. A third step within and I lost the footing. A moment later, I was deep in it. "Yet the only dirt on this crag and I find a need to wear it upon myself." 'Twas not enough to just fall within the muck, but I came from it covered upon the same as all that be mine and shook from fear.

Such was I, then, to remain upon me knees. I had a want to keep my sword ever at the ready. Alas, it kept me from a good balance; and I'd suffered of it twice. I sheathed the thing, praying I would not need it upon the next bit of path. Me head thought of the inside of the keep being just as unsteady as the out. I begged all that was I were wrong.

Upon the far side of the nasty quagmire, I found level
ground enough to bring myself back upon me feet. I stood nearest a
wall. One that opened a hundred cubits up. A small window, far
beyond my reach. The keep was round about and as tall as any
other. I should have to find another entrance. I moved towards the
yet to be seen wall farthest out, nearer the open sea. The shale
became less, the ground had more rock, moiety from the
preponderant of the keep itself. Age of the monstrous ziggurat was
such as I had not encountered. A thousand years, quite possibly
more. Upon nigh scrutiny, it seemed such that barely withstood the
fierce coast winds. Yet it did. As the beasts I'd chanced upon since
my exodus from Ementior, each were captive to unknown
possibilities. This great acropolis appeared no less the repudiation.

The great keep seemed to have the ramparts jutting forth
from several, what looked to be, desultory paths. I concluded that
they had once been intrinsic walls themselves instead of simple
fortifications. I looked back upon the shore. "'Twas a part of the
land once. This, a king's home. Perhaps." Time and rough seas
wore the connections away. "Knowledge of such shan't be of any
help." I continued my course around the far wall, searching for an
ingress.

◆ ◆ ◆

It was that the hole with which I could find the insides of
the beast (for I now thought of the keep in that way) came at such a
length that I had better to have begun my traipse to the far side and
saved not just the bout of the travel, but the slip to the water, the
visage of the seeker's bones, and, indeed, the dip into the plashet.
And the conclusionary stench that was now my own self. Of which
I feared could allude my antagonist to my presence, so ending this
before I truly even laid my eyes upon the chalice. Yet I pushed on.

I fought me own brain to hone in upon the duty at hand. I did find myself notably distracted at the thought of success. How long had the thing been here, awaiting its theft from the great Dentibus Igni? A hundred years? Nay, a thousand? Old as the keep was? Was it that this keep were a part of a castle to which the dragon himself, was responsible for the destruction of? Had he chosen it thence? Was the chalice a part of that castle's treasury? I did not like so thinking for it made me less wary. I began to hum the melody of a bygone song that I ne'er knew the words of. A slight repose, near mute. It did, indeed, assist my converge.

I disposed for the jaunt into what was a dark, most foreboding place. The hole I would wander through was a scant two cubits wide and less than that to the prominence. 'Twas a clutch to enter. Once within, I could yet see as a divvy had come loose from the planchment overhead and a good deal of light fell inside. No doubt the course that Dentibus Igni used to move about.

The light did lend what I needed to see. Yet better than I had wished. Upon my ingress, I smelled upon the wind that which was more yet putrid than myself. I feared it was the dragon himself; but in short turn, I saw the begetter of the stench. The rotted flesh of an oger-like body lay off a few cubits just within the full gloss from the fog-shrouded sunlight breaking within the keep. I needed not to muckrake the thing to know what it was and why it lay as it did. As the skeleton within the sea, this was a victim of the single denizen. Whether he fell to a stone mislaid or outright ripping of one's innards, it was Dentibus Igni's work. I drew my sword, slowly, silently from its scabbard.

The walls were of dark, wet stone. And they reached upon the sky. It was that none ever returned to explain the whereabouts of the chalice. From without, much as the distance to cover had seemed piddling, the keep seemed meager. Yet, the inners were vast. Markedly so as I had yet to have been there.

I moved toward the closest wall and meant to remain near it. Such would grant me a greater idea of my bearings and the egress when I was wont to do so. The remainder of the room was as the wall I huddled near (yet fought to tarry from so much as brushing it – it did cause ever so slight of me a gag), dank, wet, and mired of mire. As much like the pond I'd crawled about. It did, indeed, have an awful smell of it.

A deep whiff of the wall and myself and I found them to be of such harmony (if I dare to use such a word for such a thing), I could scarcely tell them apart. I contended the absolute revulsion of my nares. Were it the smell of the walls and myself or the rotting flesh steps off? I held the contents of me maw in check as I could. The beast (the dragon) would slumber if Timens were of a mind to be honest. I prayed he were.

The chamber of which I had entered was narrow and short for about 20 steps. It cornered there to either way and opened to a grand room that extended up to the ceiling. That which had the gape vast enough for Igni to proceed from and to. I suspected it to be his bedchamber, yet he was naught about. Upon the far wall, the light reflected upon a shape set back within the oozing bulwark. The great room sat betwixt it and myself. Though the winged monster was none about, it was a good court across. All of which I would be bared to any that could see. Were I to know that Igni weren't about, a moment and I would be there. There upon which I was certain were the chalice itself.

Within further scrutiny I found the immense room to be what was once a place of kings. The court of royalty. From the walls hung shards of tapestry and décor. The edgings of the floor strewn with rotting paintings and furniture. And yet more carcasses. Of both knight and animal. Most were such that I could not discern either one. This great beast relished its deeds. Such that the room seemed to be of that purpose. Where it kept the spoils. Had it thought in such a way. As a man might retain memorial to his conquests.

Or, mayhaps, he be such a lazy baggins, he left them be post devours.

As I looked closer, through the stench that was so that I covered my mouth and nostrils with the bag the old man had given me, the animals were odd. What remained of them, to that end at least. "Sea creatures." I spoke softly. 'Twas a biting question in me head. Why the old man had remained such a short jaunt up the shore. Why the monster had not tracked him about and eaten him. "This monster lives from the sea." I whispered of him. "He kills the knight, yet eats of the brine."

I continued my ingress and looked about me to find the lair of this beast. I was, indeed, within it. There were none other rooms. "He feeds." This came unto me suddenly and the boldness of meant that I was alone. But for moments only. He could return any second.

I sheathed my blade and bound with all in myself to the far wall where, indeed, the chalice sat upon a pedestal within a small alcove pushed into the slimed stone wall. The chalice took my breath. As I gazed upon it, it seemed to scintillate and give about its own light. As though the sun lit upon it suddenly. It were tall, over half a cubit. Gold of its whole, set with rubies, emeralds, sapphires, and more round about it. I was mesmerized, yet only a moment as I yanked if from its place and shoved it forthwith into the weaved bag.

I readied to go, but was struck by the spectacle there. The pedestal were covered by an old fabric. The chalice had sat so long, the cordon that it left appeared fresh. That which was out from the base of the chalice was old, dusty and wholly faded. It had no sight to it and looked as the rest about it: grey, black, and relic. Yet that which was 'neath the chalice, clean and new. It had the selfsame archetype as the bag I carried. That which the old man, Timens, gave me. I had naught the time to look about for more understanding. I turned and dashed as my life meant for it (which it, indeed, did) to the entrance I had used. I was certain there were a better way, but I had not the time to seek it out.

The small anteroom of which I came were a step up. Thus I had forgotten and found myself, in my haste and the lessening light, falling headlong into the muck that was the floor. Such had been upon the stone walk that it might have been more ooze than stone. I pulled about, worrying that the chalice may be damaged. My realization that it mattered none at that point, I bolted upon my feet and continued to the break in the wall.

Upon my egress, I turned to the adverse of which I came. Me mind cogitated that would be an easier route and included the most of the keep. This would give myself greater cover as I took to the shale-encrusted island. With, as I thought, judicious movement, I boldly took upon my return the openness of the main of the island. With such that the dragon was not about and I would be able to pick the easiest path. If such did exist there on Mortem.

The "easier" path did exist. Yet was not easy at all. I stumbled upon this and that. In my haste, I was upon the ground much. I gained me feet and continued. At last the boat was in sight. Yet upon the noise so constant of the sea, I heard something I had yet to hear. I refused a pause to investigate as I was certain of what

I heard be that of a great winged beast pressing inward to Insula Mortem. The feeding appeared to be done with.

I looked not back upon him. *Should do me no good*, I thought. I found myself upon the dock and lay graciously into the bow of the boat upon my back in angst that I would not be seen. The bag aside, I reached over me to pull the rope and begin my trip back to the shore. After pulling the slack, the tiny boat began to move. Yet nary a space as I had forgone the noose about the dock's pylon. Thus I was forced to sit about and yank it loose. As I did such I saw the black beast winging over the keep. It made no noise but the great beating of the air about it. I proceeded with me plan to lay in the boat and pull the rope.

I heaved and drug with such that my arms felt as though they were being removed. Suddenly, the boat stopped. I feared it had snagged on a rock or some water monster; but indeed, it had completed its route. I sat up watchful. I was yet alone.

Upon the dock I went to Longwise. He whiffed me filth and reared. "'Tis me, you oaf." I mounted him and reined him to turn. As I did, I watched the great Dentibus Igni float upon the fleshly wings up from the confines of the keep. He was, indeed, a grand sight to behold. From him came a sound as I had ne'er heard, nor shall imagine again. That roar was such that I still hear it ringing about me fool head. And the dreams. As such a nightly thing.

I reared Longwise and pulled him about to scatter up the trail. Yet nary a dozen cubits I had ridden than I spied Caducus upon Gallant in his greatest gallop to me. His sword drawn. I reached to pull me own. His true colors upon him now, I saw I would defend the chalice from him now that I'd had it. Yet, I had no sword. Me scabbard were empty.

I thought a moment back upon the traipse from the keep. It no doubt lay upon the floor in the anteroom from whence I fell of the step and into the slime that was such. I remained stoic, nonetheless. I should knock him from the saddle with the chalice as a boulder within a bag. So I prepared and secured the gather rope to me wrist and begun a swing to match his arrival at me.

Such distracted as I was by Caducus' charge, I had forgotten Igni's plan to return the chalice from me dead body. I watched Caducus closely as he came upon me. I swung and swung the bag. The swinging was as such more than I had expected that it created a breeze. Then suddenly a wind as Caducus and Gallant turned just so that they remained from reach. A moment more and I would lay dead at the clutches of the dragon I had forgotten sought me life.

Yet the instance passed as I had not imagined. The charge of Caducus and his loyal steed was not to me. The moment was that I was consumed upon my own accomplishment and therefore thought of nothing but that. Over me head, the silent wind that I felt was the beating of massive, scaly wings. To which belonged Dentibus Igni. Black and ugly. He descended on me to take my life and return his chalice forthwith under the cacophony of his monstrous baying.

Upon this understanding, I waited in contemplation of his teeth and fire. I looked not into his face. I sat upon my horse. I felt not even the desire to charge off. I looked upon the path of sand that led on farther up the hillside. For such a brief moment, I recalled all those who had loved me. Including Caducus. He was a good friend and a good knight. *I should like to have met his King,* I thought.

The wait for the attack upon me breech was interminable. It was at that time that I gathered it was not coming. I turned about in my saddle to find that Caducus' charge was, indeed, in my defense of the beast. That which, upon the word of fable Timens, could not be dispatched by any means. And of which began a screech that I would nary thought possible from a monster as he. He hovered about us, clutching to his chest. Caducus had shoved his sword upward to the dragon as he plunged at myself. In so doing, the tip of his sword slid up under the thick, unpierceable scales. The dragon roared in a death bawl and continued a fight to rise. He was failing.

I bound from my steed and ran to Caducus. "My dear fellow..." I screamed above the dragon's bedlam. He had rote off of Gallant and stood ready to fight more. With what, I did not know. His sword remained within the chest of Igni. Of which, continued to clutch at what was now his undoing: the sword in him. He began to back wing and push away from us. Such caused him to flip upon his back and plummet the 25 or 30 cubits to the rocky ground next to the dock. His roaring grew louder. He lay upon his back, flailing about as a cockroach in its throes of death.

We came upon him, slow and wary. He looked at us. 'Twas not just an animal. There were recognition within his eyes. He roared a last time as the crash upon the shore of the greatest wave. And he was done.

It was that I had done what no knight had. Of which I knew. My name would surely be written upon the annals of time within my kingdom. I should think the king himself would grant me the order of something all would see. So abounding with what I had done, I scarcely recalled the man beside me who was the reason I breathed.

And such thrust his hand upon my shoulder, as a brother would. "Dear me, you stink as the rot of a fish dock. What have you been about?" He yelled over the yet strident ocean.

"A bog of unimaginable size. And substance." I laughed.

"'Twas a great thing, brother. You will be commended for this!" And pointed to the bag in my hand.

"Yes. Indeed." I said. "Yet, my dear man, naught for you, I should lay there, cold and bereft of life. And that beast," I pointed to Dentibus Igni, "He should have this and back into the keep."

"'Tis who I am. Your..." As the knight spoke, he fell upon the sand and underbrush. "...friend."

I knelt quickly to his side. I now saw the blood that drained from beneath his tunic. From the amount, a great gash, from the beast's claw no doubt, had been opened. Despite the sturdy mail that he wore. "You foolish, foolish soul. I turned upon you from the words of a stupid, old man, yet you brought me enemy down at the price of thine own life." I found tears coming from my eyes. "Why? Why would you do such a noble thing for such an imbecile?"

I pulled him up to sit there in the sand. He granted upon myself a beleaguered smile. For a breath I believed he to be only weakened. "'Tis a fair thing I have done for you. 'Tis a fairer thing He has done for you. In immensity. And grander still." He gargled around blood within his mouth.

"He? What are you talking about?" I begged.

"My King. He only wishes to meet you..." His eyes closed. 'Twas the last he spoke.

I shook him. "Caducus? Caducus?"

◆ ◆ ◆

I led Longwise up the sandy trail with Gallant bearing his master as well in tow. The old man, Timens, stood from the bench we had eaten from. "Ahh, the poor lad. I told him not to run to danger. Such is the foolishness of..."

"Silence your tongue, old man. Lest I should extract it from you!" I covered my anger as much as my heart could muster. I tied the two horses to a bush and turned to the now defensive cretin. "There be a thing or two you mayhaps have left from your knowledge of the beast and that keep."

"What dost thou need now? You have defeated the dragon and fetched the chalice." He looked upon the bag in my hand. "Might I see it? Hold it? 'Tis all I require. You may return it to your king."

"Who are you?" I demanded.

"Timens. It is that I thought I had told you." He gave with a fearful smile.

"Dost you still thinkest me a fool with all that has happened upon this day? I shall run you through for you falsehoods!" I drew the sword I had in my scabbard. One that did not fit well as it was such that Caducus had and used to slay Dentibus Igni. Yet it came easily into my hand, the blood of the dragon still on the blade.

"Wait, no. Please, m'lord. I have done you no ill." He swore.

"No, you did indeed. For you put doubt in me of Caducus. You broke what took grand and life to build." I grew angrier and pointed the sword at him.

"I played upon what was already there. Your existing doubt, my boy." He went from calling myself lord to boy.

"You do it more so even now." I refused to pursue the matter further. Something bothered me. I held the bag up. He reached for it, and I pulled it back.

"Please. I wish to see it." He begged.

"'Twas an odd thing. This cup sat upon something gravely familiar." I leaned toward him, the sword edging closer from my one hand and the bag farther in my other. "Why do you have a sack of the same cloth that the chalice sat upon?"

He backed away and dropped again upon the bench. It was then that I saw his entire garb was all of the same pattern. Albeit, quite faded. A striped purple and dark blues. He looked down upon it. He stood again and walked to where the greatest view there was of the keep below. He strained to see the carcass of the dragon.

"Over a thousand years ago, that island was part of the shore. It held a grand castle." He returned to the bench.

"I had surmised something of that." I said.

"There were there at that time a great king. Powerful. An army that conquered all before them. He had treasures only thought of.

"In time, he became...hardened. Mean. He began to use his power for things evil.

"The dragon came to settle that which the king had done to his own kingdom. His knights went out to murder all that which had wings to fly." He looked up to me. "It is said, they were ne'er evil until the king of this place became their enemy. But that is not really known."

"And?" I pressed.

"I am the last of his lineage. 'Twas that I could ne'er find a mate, so none would carry on. The one, last treasure that the king had was the Chalice of Tribute. It has been called many things. The Cup of Glory. The Gratitude Grail. The *Calicem Bonitatem*. It became the representation of strength and challenge. And my own greatest failure.

""Twas that I trained as a knight that I might take it for myself. That I would retrieve it. Afore now, I am but the only to return from the island." His head drooped. "In my shame, I ran. The dragon came to me and knew me. He knew who I was. So it were that I was allowed to remain of the living and watch as knight after knight came to take that which was mine and give their lives in pursuit."

"So you remain the coward you ever were." I spat at him. I looked back at the keep in the distance. "Stay. You shan't live a long life now. There is nothing for you to hope for."

"I suppose." He said.

I untied the horses and left him there. 'Twas a truth. I had not the knowledge of the years he'd remained, waiting for just a chance to see the trinket I now carried. For the briefest moment I thought of giving it to him as my future was no longer certain. But for the then, I decided that perhaps, in time, he will come to doubt what I had in the sack and muster the wherewithal to return to the keep and see, now that the dragon were no threat, for himself what he ran from.

◆　◆　◆

It was in me to carry my friend home. To Albus Civitatus. Yet that way would hold time and, possibly, more danger. So to the Manor of Opulentus I traveled. In hopes of a solemn ending for dear Caducus.

I spent one night upon the hill above the shanty. A soft night with sand for my palette. I had not the desire to eat and built no fire. Was such a night that I only watched the grand lights of the heavens quiver and blaze. Grandest of all before and since. As though my dear brother were celebrated.

When I made it to the manor the next morn, young Alium was busy with learning the workings of the manor. Many of the servants, both freemen and serfs, remained without concern. She was well known to be a heart much as her father had been. But some refused to serve those which had served.

As the manor showed in the distance, I came off Longwise and led him and dear Gallant upon foot. A rider was dispatched out to me. He halted myself at a distance. He was one that I had not met, nor even seen. "Upon whom dost thou call?"

"I am Miratus. To see Lady Alium." There was not any that I saw different than which was on my first visit. But I could not see within.

The soldier smiled and immediately bowed in the saddle. "My lord, she will be elated." He looked past me to Gallant and his load. "Is this Sir Caducus?" I nodded. His smile left, and he turned his ride back towards the manor. "Follow me, sir." Likewise, he lighted off his mount and walked. A show of honor.

Alium was notified of my presence and came to the front of the manor to greet me. She wept at the sight of my friend. "What happened, m'lord?" She asked.

"He gave his life to save mine." I thought of those who had a moment or more in me heart. Those who birthed me. Those who trained me. Those I had passed and known. None had done for me as he had.

The magistrate had, indeed, become her assistant and was there. She told me of the struggles and glories that had transpired in the last day since we had left. Much had come about in such a time.

"It shall be as I had said." The magistrate told me. "A difficult battle lay before us, but we are nary alone."

The manor, having been in place for a time, had a small field that was encompassed about by a stone wall. It was for those of whom had passed. Alium did my friend the honor of placing him beside the plot that had been reserved for her father. "I have dispatched some to retrieve his body. He shall have the place upon my father's right."

I stayed one night and vowed to return someday. Amabilia's smile was ne'er far from my mind. Caducus' sword were to be me own now. I would mend my scabbard to match it. I asked Alium to care for Gallant. His further belongings were meant to be within his own Kingdom. So it was that I would bring them myself unto Albus Civitatus.

"Fear thou not; for I am with thee: be not dismayed; for I am thy God: I will strengthen thee; yea, I will help thee; yea, I will uphold thee with the right hand of my righteousness."
Isaiah 41:10

Chapter 10
Albus Civitatus

"And you found your way here?" Basil said, his face looking of wonder upon the long chronicle of Sir Miratus.

"Indeed, my friend." Miratus replied. He glanced backward. "'Twas a slight path back there. Very narrow. Such that I nearly missed it. Indeed, I did. Twice. Thus the need to recall of Caducus and my first meet."

"'Twas quite a journey." Basil leaned towards him and sniffed. "You have bathed. That is good." He smiled.

The knight laughed. "Yes. I have come with a new grasp upon foul odor. Especially, that of my own."

"How long did it take to journey here from Alium's manor?" The man queried.

"Not but a fortnight. That which took us from the ogre, Fastus, and Rubropontem to Inlitora were four, at least. Maybe even five." He looked about. The two ambled upon a slight road that sat at the edge of a great, green meadow to their left. It seemed to stretch many great leagues unto imposing, dark mountains. A dense forest went off to their right. "I miss the fool. I shan't ever understand as to why he'd feel to defend myself with his life."

"Seems as though he'd done so before Mortem. Before the dragon." The other observed. Miratus nodded agreement.

They rode on, and the knight remained silent. At length, he glanced at the other. "What of those yon mountains? Are they yet within this Kingdom?" He desired, after the long narrative of his friend and of how they met and fought together, to move onto other things.

The man glanced at the majestic rising. "Yes. All you can see here is within the Albus Civitatus. This Kingdom."

"It is such as I have ne'er seen. Such beauty."

Miratus pointed back over his shoulder to the breech of the trail. "'Twas a good thing that I met you back yonder. I'd have soon been lost." He said, inferring the many trails that wandered aimlessly.

"I am glad, as well." Basil replied.

The knight pointed to the trail before them. It was still narrow but was improving. The land about them continued to become more beautiful and lush. "Do you plan to remain upon the way to the City?"

"Indeed. I know the way there quite well. I will lead you there." Basil nodded.

"How long to this Albus Civitatus?"

"We are there. All about us is the land of Albus Civitatus. 'Tis all the Kingdom of such." He smiled as he spread his arms wide. "Yet, the city is a bit along. We should take sight of it within a day or two. Shall be another upon us, though, before we arrive." Basil replied. "So, a certain three days. Perhaps a little more."

"Very well."

"It is such that I happen to know this grand hero you told me of. This Caducus." Basil spoke.

Miratus pulled Longwise up. "Sir? And you only say so now?"

"Pardon, please. He is an august friend; I enjoyed listening to your candor of him. I shouldn't have given you influence to be less than forthright of the man by you knowing he and I were close." Basil said.

Miratus nudged Longwise, and the journey resumed. "I suppose." He looked the man over there upon his tiny donkey colt. "He was..." Miratus nodded his head to keep the shame of tears from sight. "He was indeed a good friend." He raised his head. "'Twas that I tried to speak of something other." He sighted upon the mountains to look away from his companion.

"'Tis hard to lose someone who had such love and honor about them." Basil enjoined. He looked at Miratus. "I know 'tis a burdensome thing, but should you like to know more of him?"

Miratus refused to look at the man. There was an air of him that the knight relished. His presence were that like Caducus, and he drew to him quickly. He had yet to understand it from the knight whom had given his life in his stead. He was less comprehensive of it now with Basil. Remaining his gaze upon the distant hills, he replied, "Shouldst you give me rise to weeping, say nothing of it. But, indeed, I would beg to know more of the man."

"Yes, dear Sir, all is betwixt us alone." He smiled.

"Then, proceed on."

"As you wish." He breathed in and pulled the long tunic he wore back a bit and began. "Caducus was not of the Albus Civitatus. The Great White City was not the place of which he

commenced life. Indeed, the youngster came from another
kingdom much as your own.

"He was wide eyed and ready to save all that needed so.
And there were many. He foraged the land about him and learned
the ways of rectitude and goodness. It was such that he held, and all
could see the peace that is such a part of this beautiful land."

"He spoke of the King as though he knew Him like a
brother." Miratus interrupted. "Nay, as a Father. Yet One that was
close, upon every day of his breath."

"He did, indeed. They were close." Basil smiled.

Miratus shook his stodgy head. "How is such? How could
the King of such a land know each..." He drifted off.

"Know each?" Basil enquired. "Finish your words, Sir
Miratus."

Miratus reined in Longwise and gazed to the mountains still.
"Within my kingdom, I traveled near two days to come to the
palace. There, they placed my quest upon me. A simple one, yet it
came to be, as you know, a great one that should have had me torn
upon black shale.

"But did this king say to me, "Luck to you, young knight?""
He petitioned to Basil. "Not at all. The dull-witted functionaries
laughed at the thought that he had the time to engage myself." He
looked down at the ground there next to Longwise. "I was merely a
member of their list of those easier to shove off to some duty
mayhaps I should solve and benefit a master that rarely spoke upon
the heart of one country-ridden knight. Of no repute, no ballyhoo."

"And no importance?" Basil asked.

Miratus looked up to the man there on the little animal. For the first time, he looked at him closely. He was that of Miratus' age. He sat on the small steed and looked as though he was most comfortable with whatever station he'd be upon. But he did not have anything that would seem of much station at all. "Yes. Of no importance." He laughed. "To which I cannot say I should expect any."

He looked to the road before them and returned to the slow cadence along it. "Of truth I have accomplished nary previous to this month and more of enterprise and peril. 'Twas that I had in mind that the king should see me now. Possibly upon my return. Yet I am inquisting as to returning at all."

"Where then?" Basil asked.

"I doubt my franchise. I should think on it for a time." He spread his hands. "There is much to see." He laughed. "And serfs to be freed. I should like to be in that fight." He looked at Basil. "You, dear sir, what do you consider on that subject?"

The man smiled in response. "That no man should be a slave except to goodness."

Miratus looked away to the trail before them. He leaned forward to the ears of Longwise. "You, big fellow. You hear that? That is utter wisdom." He leaned back upon the saddle and looked at Basil. "Then such is settled. I shall return to the Opulentus Manor and assist to take up arms in the fight for the freedom of all serfs."

"I scarce can think of a nobler deed, my friend." Basil smiled.

Miratus withdrew his sword (that which was once Caducus') and raised it straight into the air. "It is then, thus I decree. My most singular quest shall encompass the remainder of my life. To set the enslaved upon the world, loosed and free!"

Basil applauded. "Indeed, my friend. 'Tis nothing I could think upon better for you to put yourself within."

"Should you enjoin me, 'twould be a dignified and lofty purpose to die for?" Miratus smiled.

"Haha, your levy routine should stand a few improvements. Yet I shall consider it to heart." Basil replied.

Though the beauty and the majesty of the land enthralled Miratus, he derived the lack of others. He did not ask Basil, but it seemed at odds of anything normal.

Another hour and he thought to the subject of his late companion. "As I had sought earlier, do return to the tale of Caducus. How was it that he lived?"

"Indeed." Basil pondered a moment. "As you had said, your kingdom left you with such a heart of no value. 'Tis ne'er been such here. All that are about are of great importance. Young Caducus came to know that, and it spurred him all the more.

"Yet, he ne'er left here. He was that which his King had called him to be, but only here in a place that all agreed to his thinking.

"Notwithstanding so, his life was grand and a beauty who saw him and loved him came to be his wife." Basil said.

"Wife? The fool ne'er once postulated of a damsel." Miratus said, scratching his head.

"'Tis the truth. Yea, and two offspring of beauty as well." Basil added.

"Not so, you say? 'Tis that I should come to meet them. They must needs of the reason their beloved mate and father shan't return." Miratus added, sadly.

"I should think it good to do such." Basil said. "That is, to say that you should meet them."

Miratus nodded as Basil returned to his narrative. "So it was, a year upon the birth of that spry little one that he concluded his was a lot of eloquence and soft.

""I shall go to that what is without the Albus Civitatus and see that which does not know this peace that I do. There be at least one that needs what I have." Basil smiled at Miratus.

"So it was true, he was there to seek that of myself?" The knight asked.

"Yes. But do not think ill of the man. He was genuine until his life was taken for yours."

Miratus smiled, yet a tear dribbled about down his cheek. "I shall think no less of him." He gingerly wiped the dampness from himself and looked again to the road.

Before them a small river crossed. "Upon the far shore is a well-used flat of which I have camped a few nights. It should be a good place for such tonight." Basil pointed.

"Indeed."

Miratus left the camp upon its readiness and sought small game for food. He returned as dark began to fall with a diminutive hare. He found Basil waiting for it. They sat upon logs that had been gathered and ate together. "'Tis better than ol' Caducus' meat. He could fight. He was smart. He was kind to which none compared, save this King he always spoke of. Yet the man's best cookery was mud from a banshees gut." The two laughed. They laughed not at the man nor of the man, but at what the knowledge of having known the man had given them.

◆ ◆ ◆

Basil woke to find Miratus stirring and rebuilding the fire. It was yet dark. "You rise early." He said to him

The knight spoke without taking his eyes from what he was doing. "'Tis hard to rest. My friend seems to be always upon me mind. And that beast..." He rose to his feet. "I shall fetch something for breakfast."

Basil rose and continued to succor the fire. He went about to locate branches and wood to build it up. Yet a short time and he had the fire burning hard. Miratus returned again with another small hare. "They do grow bigger in this land, my friend." Basil smiled.

"Indeed, I hope." Miratus replied, handing it to Basil. "This will suffice as of now, though."

They ate, led their steeds to a bit of grass, and were about their way as dawn came full to the land about them.

"Such a difficult thing to leave behind." Miratus said, at length.

Basil knew that of which he spoke. "It is toilsome to lose a friend."

"Of certain, it is." Miratus stared down to his pommel. The beauty and wonder of the surrounding country made it difficult to think of his sadness and look at it both. "'Tis difficult to think of what I could have done a moment quicker and not lost the man."

"You mean to have gotten out of the keep faster? To not have hung up the boat? Not have slipped in the pond of stink?" Basil spoke with insight Miratus did not expect. They both smiled at the reference to the puddle without the keep.

"Yes. Had I been a moment farther, mayhaps that beast would not have caught me. And dear Caducus would be here, with me now." Miratus intoned, tapping on the bag that held Caducus' chattels and goods.

"Yes, and your suspicions of him would remain."

Miratus pulled Longwise and stopped. "Such a truth I had not considered." He resumed the cantor after the short pause. "Caducus spoke upon his last breath. It was something I had not understood." He breathed. "Nor do I yet."

"'Tis a fair thing I do. But a fairer thing He does?" Basil asked.

Miratus looked upon Basil. "Yes. That." He raised his hands. "How is that such a thing is true? Were he speaking as such or did he incline something other than plain speech?"

"You thought it great that he had done a thing as that. To give his life in your stead. Yet he gave his last utterance to point you towards his King. Is that which you ask?" Basil said.

"Surely."

Basil smiled. "'Tis a nobleman's thought." He looked to their trail ahead and plodded onward. "Young Caducus went forth to do that which was upon his heart. To serve the King. In such service that one has chosen, there is a part that becomes as the One who is served. Caducus did as he did for he was like unto his King." He stopped his speech a moment and looked at Miratus. "Do you understand?"

"He was who he was because of He who had the greatest mark upon him. His King." Miratus replied. "An imprint of dignity and virtue. Indeed, truly a nobleman's thought."

Basil continued. "You see a part. But not yet all." He continued their trek along the edge of the woods. He pointed off towards the mountains. "The trees there on the top of the mountain are not the same as these here in the valley. They live from the minerals higher up. They endure the cold more. They are formed and persuaded of that which they live from. Caducus was the same. Yet he understood a greater truth." They came upon a small stream. They dismounted and allowed the beasts to lounge and drink.

Taken by the sight of the far reaching mountains that Basil had pointed to, Miratus stood looking to them. "I should like to climb them. To look back to here, from there."

"You will. And it will be magnificent."

The knight looked back to Basil. "And this greater truth?"

"He did not come upon you because he sought goodness. He was not scouting the highway in search of a stranger who would be a friend he could possibly die to save. No indeed, he followed that which his King led him upon."

"And this King, He put Caducus upon me? In particular?" Miratus asked.

"In such a way, yes. Caducus was sent. He did not just go, but went upon a mission he knew not the details of."

"He was trusting." Miratus commented with a queer drift in his voice.

"Indeed. Yet, did you not go upon a quest trusting with no knowledge of your time? Would you return and how many years forth would it be?" Basil said.

"'Tis true. Yet I had a quest that had an end." Miratus pointed out.

"As did Caducus."

Miratus waited for Basil to finish. But he added no more. He took the small, colorful bag from his saddle and held it up. "'Tis my end. This, this chalice was my quest. I can hold it. I can see it." He reattached it to his saddle. "What, pray tell, were Caducus' end? His quest?"

"That, my friend, is more than a simple trinket." Basil said, knowing that it would irk Miratus to be beholding to such a thing.

For it was not simple, this "trinket" had great meaning to it. It would take him to places in his kingdom that no one else had seen. He still dreamed of the triumphal entry he would have as he brought the famed Chalice of Tribute to his king. "'Tis an insult that you bestow upon me. This is hard fought and won."

"Yes, at the cost of our friend's life. Hard fought, indeed."

"I did not intend to belittle his sacrifice..." Miratus said quickly.

"No, indeed. But it is of a truth that you say sacrifice. That was it." Basil said.

"I fear that we have missed and wandered about." Miratus pointed to the breech with his thumb. "What is it said of Caducus, then?" He asked.

"I shall put it plainly." He pulled the donkey up and stopped. "Caducus was as his King were. He was because his King was such. Yet, his quest did not have a name unto him. He only obeyed the call to go.

"In so going, he fell upon you; and you see the tale from there. It is, though, that the King dear Caducus emulated and loved knew of the adventure. He knew of the future for both Caducus and the friend he'd meet and become a brother to. He knew of the one whom Caducus would finally sacrifice his whole for. He, the King, Caducus' King, He knew of you before the joining together of closest brothers in arms." He concluded, breathing outward. He urged the colt forward.

Miratus, who had reined in Longwise at the behest of the other's stop, sat there in the saddle, thinking hard through that which the other had said. The trail ahead curved about, and he looked to see Basil was disappearing about such. He spurred on his mount, and they caught up.

They remained silent as the knight consumed all that had been said. He found it to be balderdash immediately. But as moments changed and the day grew on, he considered the story as a whole and saw that, indeed, it seemed to fit within the parameters. "So the obedience that Caducus had, goaded him to me."

Basil breathed deeply. "'Tis that you are stubborn." Miratus knew not whether to grin or frown. "Such can be a good thing. In the right moment." They moved on a bit, and Basil spoke again. "One must obey their king. Yet he who *desires* to do so has a greater kinship. He did not obey the call to go forth of a need due the hierarchy of the King. It was his love for his King. He desired to do as his King asked."

"Love? 'Tis an odd way to describe that which is between a man, knight or otherwise, and a king. He is king. He need not be loved. Only..." He slowed his speech to a stop. Then added, "Obeyed."

"Within your kingdom, you were brought to be given a quest. Had you disobeyed?" Basil asked.

"'Twould not be considered. I should think it the last of which I would commit to action. A hanging, mayhaps?"

"Yes. But had you wished not to go upon this quest, would there be a way about it? One that you would live?" Basil asked.

"None that I know. I am certain had I not responded, some would find their way to me; and I would be forced." He replied.

"And should you know that you would fail? That your life would be forfeit? Perhaps that which the old man told you that none had returned, would you have sojourned of love for your king?" The local said.

"Is there a pertinence to this?" Miratus replied, weary of the question.

"Only that Caducus knew of such possibilities, yet went. His King ne'er forcing such upon him, merely asking." Basil acquiesced.

At length, the two found themselves entering a small village. Not more than a dozen huts were strewn about. Children played, and Basil was recognized by some of the people. They found their way to the front of a small eating house. The sun had warmed, and they took time to eat inside. Miratus had not felt tranquil in some time. His focus had been, from the moment he was called up to the palace, upon the chalice.

"Thy countenance is light. You seem content and joyful." Basil said as they ate.

Miratus merely smiled and continued the meal.

Once they were done, their horses watered and fostered, they continued upon the journey to Albus Civitatus. The White City.

The way wound about, gained ground, and rose uphill. The two traversed several more villages. They seemed to be common. Many were as large as Rubropontem. Some even larger. But most were small. All of them had the same thing in common: Basil was known by many people.

"You appear to be well known abouts." Miratus mentioned as they began to set for camp near a small brook.

"I travel often. I find a lot of joy in seeing friends." He smiled.

Once a fire was lit and they worked on dinner, Miratus spoke, "I have a thought."

Without looking up, Basil replied, "And that is?"

"This King. The One who Caducus was so fond of. Wouldst he meet with me?"

Basil smiled. "Oh, of a certain."

"As Caducus knew him and as he was the man's cavalier, I should think he'd want the remnants of his own gentleman." Miratus said.

"Yes, indeed. I know for certain He shall."

The paladin stirred the coals and meandered. "I must say, this King is not as any I have heard of. I am but a farm boy with a title and have confessed to you all I have frequented. My travels be light. But nary another have I even heard tell of be as He is."

"He is as no other. That is how He should be. It is how all kings should be. Yet, he the only of such a heart."

Miratus pointed at the striped bag that lay on the ground. "Well, then, maybe even that. He should do good with such a trinket."

"My friend, your heart remains in a choice direction. Yet I doubt He is in need of even that beauty." Basil assured him.

Miratus seemed hurt. "And tomorrow, we arrive?" He asked.

"Indeed. Yet late. The spires shall be in view by mid-morning."

"It is then we shall see if He desires such." The knight said. He rose from his sit and found the bedroll from Longwise. He laid it out with not a word. His demeanor slight and dis-use for Basil some evident. He wanted to be wanted. It was something of which, he felt, must be paid for by his own. The gentle Basil resisted words, understanding. He too found it a good time to sleep.

◆　◆　◆

Upon the morn, Miratus had felt the impasse gone and bothered it no more. They conversed a bit and found some light fare left from the night before to dispatch. Then, once more, the two gathered their slight possessions and mounted the steeds, bound for the city. Miratus upon the great Longwise, bold and brilliant. Basil gainly on the miniscule donkey colt. Miratus looked at the tiny animal numerous times as they cantered to the famed White City. He who rode seemed of much more a state than who would ride such. Not by his appearance, but by the manner to which he carried himself and the way of his conversation. *He seems regal,* the knight thought to himself.

The land before them had turned from the edge of a great open meadow to hilly and of forests. Trees of many designs and genus grew all about them. A few as tall as they upon their steeds and some that seemed beyond sight. Here and there he espied orchards, creeks, and game.

Miratus wondered back to the moment he stood upon Longwise overlooking the great City of Ementior. The busyness of it all and the drab, dull luster that so disappointed him. He looked about and saw the beauty and color of the land, then pondered that the same disillusion would rear upon them as he found the Albus Civitatus.

The two rode the way before them. It wound about climbing and settling hills and small valleys. The distant mountains were long from sight as the trees and ridges held them from view.

"Such majesty. Such amazing beauty as I have not seen." Miratus looked upon Basil. "I did not know such a place e'er existed before now."

Basil merely smiled.

A great hill lie before them. At the base a small, wayside sat. The shanty there had an open side and a counter strewn with fruit. Much kinds that Miratus had ne'er seen. As they pulled their animals up and sat off them, the man who tended the place ran from inside. "Basil! Oh, my Master. It is so good to see you!" The man, old and bent, spoke with brilliance in his eyes. He was clearly poor, yet did not speak as such. "Please, m'lord, take of this. It is the freshest. I picked it only yesterday." He offered Basil and Miratus (as though he knew him) a small wooden box each. They were filled with long, thick, black-colored berries.

"Oh dear, Colonus! Thank you! You know my love for mulberries." Basil said, gratefully.

"My good man, thank you kindly." Miratus looked at the fruit. It was, indeed, very delicious to look upon. He fished into his pocket and pulled a coin about, handing it to Colonus.

"No, no, no. This for you! You enjoy." The old man insisted. "To travel with such, I honor Him by way of honor to you!" Miratus did not understand. Yet he bowed and thanked him.

They returned to the road, now leading their rides on foot as they nibbled the mulberries. "I've ne'er had such fare. 'Tis as sweet as true love." Miratus said as they ambled. He looked at his companion. It was that he wanted to know more of the man, yet felt as though he already did. He was bearded and comely. He seemed as unremarkable as any. Miratus had presumed the man to be a fellow knight of some sort. *A knight with a tiny donkey makes little practicality*, he thought to himself. "So, dear Basil, might I enquire as to your…"

"There!" Basil smiled pointing to the distance.

Miratus turned from looking at Basil to where he pointed. They had made it to the top of the hill; and the knight had been such concerned with the berries and what the man at his side appeared to be, he scarcely knew where they were. Before them lay more rolling hills and forests. Yet their bearings had them at such height they could see beyond these. And there, distended slightly above the trees farthest, white spires rose into the blue sky. The warrior stood still, lost in thought and silent. His arms fell at his side; and the few berries that remained in the small box fell to the ground, forgotten. He could not see the whole city. Nary but the apexes, glowing as crystal.

He glanced to Basil, who stood at the reins smiling, then back to the distant scene. "'Tis a wonder. Mayhaps that I ne'er arrive there, I should be comforted knowing what I see now is genuine."

"Ahhh…but you shall." Basil assured him.

Post prodding, Basil led them farther down into another small valley. There remained many between them and the Civitatus. Miratus remained fast upon the sight he'd seen. "'Twas quite a wonder." He intoned while watering the steeds at a small stream.

As they sustained their trek, the road continued to meander back and forth. It narrowed and widened. They passed a few travelers at length. Many nodded and smiled. Some knew Basil, and some did not. Miratus did wonder at how so many could know this one man. *He did say he traveled a bit*, Miratus thought. *Perhaps he wanders this road often.*

The knight found himself easy with Basil. A willing heart to talk of all that he'd lived. He put himself to describing every detail of Patrice, his home village. Then his own, sparse chalet. The farm, as it were. Less farm and more field. He spoke more of his father and mother. Then Certus, the farm hand and friend.

"Seems of just a day or two I rode Longwise the first time." He patted the beast's neck. "He has been the most loyal of friends."

"How long has he been thus?" Basil asked.

"He was the present of me eighteenth birth celebration. My father had coaxed a breeder some distance from town. I've no idea what he traded the man." Miratus said. He looked at the donkey colt. "And what of him? What is his appellation?"

Basil looked down at the donkey. "I call him Balaam. He is loyal and gentle. Yet young with much to learn."

"Ahhh, I see. He has the earmarks of one easy to handle." Miratus remarked.

Basil nodded. "Yes, he is. And shall be all the better as he grows. He is eager."

Miratus wondered of the pace. "I do not wish to appear so keen or restless, but are you sure we will make it this day? We seem to have come a good distance with no more than trees and yet more ridge tops to account for."

"Patience, Miratus. 'Tis no more than a few furlongs remain." He smiled. "The stream we are coming about has good fish in it. I shall catch a few, and you make a fire."

"That is a splendid notion. The berries were delightful, but me barren breadbasket does rumble a bit." Miratus agreed.

'Twas but another hundred cubits, and they found the creek. The knight went about finding all he needed for a fire, and Basil found his way upstream.

At mid-afternoon they both resided upon the grassy banks, savoring the fish they had feasted upon. "Such is the soiree at the castle. The Albus Civitatus. None who come leave hungry."

"Fish?"

"Nay, my friend. Fish, beef, deer, fowl, and more. With each a trimming as you have yet to see." Basil said, smiling.

Miratus rose from the bank and patted his meager paunch. "It feels good to have a full gullet." He looked at the road and back to Basil. "Nonetheless, if such awaits us, then we be on our way." He climbed back up to the road where Longwise and Balaam awaited them as Basil joined him.

The way progressed much as it had until they found themselves at one hill that rose such that the road had to snake back and upon itself scaling to the top. They had walked the animals mostly. A slight, off-beat canter a few times. Though Miratus found himself bearably avid, he seemed content to settle back. As though Basil engaged him to be calm. Yet, he was not aware of it. The beasts took them near half way, and the two dismounted to allow a repose and continued up with reins in hand.

As they reached the summit, Basil pointed them back to the far reaches of the valley they had crossed. It was late afternoon and shadows were coming up long. "You can scarcely see it, my friend; but there, among those dark trees, there is where we met."

Miratus squinted his eyes to see. "Yes, I believe I see them." A deep breath and he took in the whole before him. As beautiful as what he had seen already, this was grander by far. Without realizing it, he began to weep.

"Sir Miratus? Are you well?" Basil asked. Though knowing yet well what caused the lament.

He stared upon the land, not eager to let the welling inundation fog his vision. He wiped his face and fought it. "'Tisn't as anything I imagined, my friend." He pointed over his shoulder with the thumb upon his right hand. "I know that behind us lay the greatest spectacle that a man can see, yet here..." He whimpered and shook. He spread his hands before him. "None can see this and not see God."

"It is such. And you, my friend, you know more than you allow yourself to see." Basil put his arm around the knight. "You are great in the kingdom."

Miratus looked upon Basil that stood so near. But he was different. He pushed back to see the Man more clearly. He wasn't Basil...

To his left he could now see the great City. He glanced at it. He looked back to Basil. Such were that he fought to take his eyes from one to the other.

The City glowed. It was, indeed, white. Yet, not white. The knight fought to understand. He looked at Basil. He now stood before him not like the commoner he'd traveled with, but a great Warrior. He still had the face of Basil, yet the remainder had changed. Like the City, He glowed. But the long flowing robe that He'd worn from the moment they had met had been replaced by a glistening garb of a grand knight. Miratus looked upon the Man. He appeared as no one he'd ever seen before.

His feet were shod and covered by silvery sabatons led into by highly polished greaves. From there up he wore a mail armor and a purest white tunic behind a silver and gold breastplate. His arms covered in the same mail leading up beneath a polished leather shoulder pauldron with a flowing white cape to his breech. Hanging from His side were the priestly sword of the ages. A scabbard of fine silver with gold inlay and, what appeared to be, a solid pearl pommel stuck out from a jewel encrusted sword handle.

Miratus stood still, breathing like the snout of a horse post a hundred furlong run. His gaze found its way to the smiling, gentle face of his Friend and traveling companion, Basil. Upon that gaze he saw what swiftly explained away all the questions his noggin had postulated that he'd failed to bring about. Above the smile, above the gentle face of Basil rested the Crown of the King. Such shock to Miratus, he could utter nothing. In truth, as a knight (or any other form) it was that the king of anything had yet to come upon him face to face. The thought of what or how to go on left him. Knowing only that this was not that which all or even few, would see upon their life, he fell to the ground. "Your...your Majesty." He said.

He feared to look at the Man. He had spoken freely of much. Now he discovered that He who Miratus had spoken so freely with was King of the Land. Of The Albus Civitatus. The King always held life or death in His grasp. *I've played the fool*, he thought. *It will be that I have been the twit, and now I shall get as I deserve.*

"Nay, dear knight. You have not been the fool. You are not a twit, and you've nothing to fear." Basil spoke.

Miratus wanted to reply but dared not. *How does he know what I think?*

"Do you remember what I told you about Caducus coming to you because his King loved you? Not because Caducus knew as he would the route or the quest that he were about?" The King said.

Without raising his head, Miratus replied. "Yes, O King. I recall."

"Then, please, stand up. Look at me." Basil said.

Miratus braved it and did look up. What he saw both bereaved and elated him. The knightly look of a king was gone, and the Basil he'd come to know stood there in his long, ungainly robe with Balaam behind him. Miratus stood.

"I am fraught with confusion." He said. Then added, "My Lord."

Basil smiled. "It is alright." He laughed. "It is that I wanted you to understand Who I Am."

"But you were a simpleton upon a young donkey for all this time..." Miratus scratched his head. "How is it that you are suddenly King, then...poof, Basil again? Is this sorcery?"

"I assure you, good knight, it is not magic." He put his arm around Miratus and began to lead him to the City.

Yet another sight to behold, the City glistened as the King had a moment before. Miratus listened as the King of Albus Civitatus explained. "You are important to me. Even though you were of another kingdom, I wanted you to know that you were important. My friend and servant, Caducus, desired to go forth and do my will. I chose him to bring my own goodness to you. His heart was to do as I required without question. I did not make him to do this; he desired it.

"He went forth as I had instructed him, and he encountered you. You became his quest. Not that you were an object of want, but that you were important to Me. He knew such was and gave to save you. Even unto his life.

"Yet afore that, he showed you My own goodness inside of him. That goodness grew to be a part of you. And your heart became changed. You were ready to throw a serf asunder as you wished. Now you desire to fight for one.

"You have seen the good in one that belongs to Me." Basil finished.

It was that poor Miratus remained as though unable to speak. He simply hung to the King, needing such to remain upright.

The Albus Civitatus grew closer. There was much goings on. He recalled his path into the City of Ementior. How the place was awash in bustling people and labor. How he fussed about to find the palace. How he was taken as just another would-be knight. Treated no more than a quaff or underling. Oft called a squire. For which he was not much more. Ridiculed at the thought that the king would bother with his attention.

Yet here, into this grand City, here in a land not his own, not even his home, he was escorted into the City by the King Himself. *How can this be?* He asked himself.

"It is because I love you. You are important to Me." Once again the King read his thoughts.

"Sire, you are no commonplace king." He fought simply to place words with one another.

Everything his own land had within it this land had, yet crosswise. The land grew more beautiful as they grew closer to the City. The colors and wonder that much greater. In short time, they found themselves nearer the City; and he saw people coming and going. They were clothed in a variety of regalia. Full of hues and tincture. They looked upon him and the Man he traveled with. They smiled, and many bowed or curtsied towards Basil.

Miratus, now walking upon his own, looked at the King. "Thou art a strange kind of King."

"He is not just a King." A man spoke up who had bowed in passing. "He's the King of Kings." Miratus looked at the man. It was that he wished to understand, yet it made scant wisdom to him.

Amid the growing crowd, he asked the King, "Why did you meet me as a commoner?"

"Had I come to you as the King you saw there on the hillside, how would you speak to Me?" He laughed. "Miratus, 'tis true I desire to be your King. Yet it is greater for me to become your Friend."

Another man stepped forward and took Miratus by the arm. "Ahh, Germanus." The King said, smiling at the man.

"Your Highness." He said to Basil. Looking back at Miratus, he spoke again. "He parades us all down these streets. We are not just a part of His kingdom, we are part of His family."

Miratus felt ill at ease. Yet not fearful. The man smiled as he let go. Basil spoke. "Come, I shall get us some tea; and you may sit."

The grand city grew up around them as they ventured farther in. Finally, they found a small building. It looked much like his home in Patrice. With steeds now tied upon the post without, they went in. Miratus carried the bag with the chalice. As well that of Caducus' tunic and matters. Basil found the means and put tea upon the stove.

"Why?" The knight asked upon sitting.

"Why do I persist in being as thou?"

"Yes...yet I have many other whys to ask as well." Miratus looked to the spotless floor.

"Yes, and many shall be answered. Maybe all, given the time." He sat opposite at the old, hand-made table. "I am King. That shan't change. I have been as a pauper and as the King. Those who know Me well, know that should I stand before them in regal attire or rags, I Am He. But I stand in a robe, simple and un-elegant. I do not need to purport that I am King always. And I wish to speak and love upon those who feed the pigs as those who abound in jewels."

The tea was served in short, and Miratus traversed his confusion. Deep within, he felt as he ne'er had. Joy and satisfaction. Yet all he'd grown to be and know from birth told him that a King is not as he saw here. "'Tis a scrumptious tea." He smiled and sipped. "My Lord."

"My name is Basil." He replied with a grand smile. "We are friends, are we not?"

Miratus rose from his chair and pulled the chalice from its bag, lighting it upon the old table. "It was that I would offer this to the King. So I do. 'Tis yours, King. To do as you wish."

Basil rose, a smile upon his face. He bent over the table and pushed the chalice back to Miratus. "'Tis yours."

"My nobility runs but to the place of knighthood. Such should remain with a lord of some sort." He pushed it back.

Basil began laughing. He continued such for a moment more. Miratus smiled. In short, they both laughed loudly. A pause to breathe and Basil spoke. "This..." He pointed to the bag that contained Caducus' belongings. "I believe that the dear knight's family would have you to take." He sat. "And wear it as your own."

"Yet he was a knight of this realm, not mine." Miratus argued.

"Then a souvenir of a great man." Basil insisted.

"And this?" Miratus pointed to the Chalice of Tribute.

"My friend, you fought to acquire it. Such is yours to grant." He smiled. "Take it and bestow it upon your king."

Miratus opened the bag and pulled the mail and tunic forth. The helmet came out as well. Greaves and gauntlets. The sword already at his side. They held his eyes as his mind wondered and reflected.

"This idea, to fight for the Lady Alium, shall you proceed?" Basil asked.

With no answer, Miratus raised the tunic, pulling it over his head and down upon himself. He pulled Caducus' sword from its scabbard and looked at Basil. "I should think it to be a grand way to spend my life. Indeed."

Basil rose again to his feet. "Indeed, my friend." He agreed, and stuck out his hand as to shake Miratus'.

"I shan't be a great grace, but it is not the end." He breathed deep, refusing the proffered limb.

"No, it is not, Sir Miratus." He pointed once more at the chalice. "And that, you shall give unto your king?"

"Yes." Miratus took the chalice from the table. He smiled at his twisted reflection in the gold. In a moment, it was struck. The seal made in his mind and heart. He grinned at Basil and turned, kneeling deftly at the feet of the King. He bowed his head, and the chalice rose in offering to Basil. "Should you accept this gift, I should know that I will fight for you. You and You alone." He raised his head and looked into the eyes of Basil. "You, My King."

**And he hath on his vesture and on his thigh a name written, KING OF KINGS, AND LORD OF LORDS.
Revelation 19:16**

Glossary:

Words	Pronunciation	Meaning
Quia Rex Meus	kwi-uh rex may-us	For My King
Miratus	Mare-a-tus	wondering
Caducus	Kad-a-cus	frail
Albus Civitatus	owl-bus chivi-totus	White City
cubit	kue-bit	approximately 18 inches
Ementior	E-ment-e-or	Lies
Bona Voluntate	Bona Volun-tate	Good intentions
Patrice	Pah-treece	Home town
Oppidville	O-pid-vil	Small town
Stolidus	Staul-a-dus	Fool
Praetus	Pray-tus	Guard
Literamet	Lit-ur-a-met	Paperwork
puer terra	pewer terra	country boy
Amica	Amee-ka	friend
Proculas	Prauk-ulas	far away
Magna Gramina	man-ya gram-eenya	great lawn
Arbitrium	Arba-tree-um	decision
Certus	Ser-tus	reliable
Fastus	Fast-us	pride
Rubropontem	Rue-bro-pon-tim	Red Bridge
et miles	eat miles	knight of
Quod perficitur per triumphum petis	Kwod per-feechur per tri-am-foom pet-is	Whatever it takes to win
Pulcher equus quaero unum elicui	pul-ker e-koos kwiro oonum eelee-kwee	beautiful horse Alone the quest I seek
ego potest hoc facere	egg-o pot-est hoke fat-charie	I can do this

Words	Pronunciation	Meaning
fatuus vobi	fa-toos vo-bee	you are a fool
plus unum sumus	plus oonum soomus	we are stronger together
foedus meum	fo-adus may-um	my confederate
unde oportet	oon-day oportay	of course
timoribus	tim-or-eebus	fears
quippe	kweep	of course
Disisderas	de-sis-dere-us	desire
usus set	use-use est	used up
duo fortissimi	doo-o for-tees-eemee	with two fighters
quidem	kee-dim	indeed
saluto	sa-looto	greeting
Bravio	bra-vee-o	gamble, prize
Antitheus	an-teeth-us	devil
Aleo	a-lay-o	gambler
miles militis quod	mise mil-ee-tus kqod	a knight is a knight
Tu solum vivis unum tempus!	too sol-um vee-vus oonum tempus	you only live once
gnome malum	nome mal-um	evil gnome
quia sermo meus miles	kwia sar-mo may-ohs mise	my word as a knight
Lucrum	loo-crum	greed
ludus	loo-dus	plainly
Lacertus	la-ser-tus	strong lizard
Sic ego dixi vobis	seek eego dick-see vobees	I told you so
iuncta	ee-oonk-ta	side by side, equal pair
amicus meus	ameek-ose may-ose	my friend
Alium	alee-um	different
Juxta Iter	uxta eeter	wayside
est qui sumus	est kwee soomus	this is who we are
advena	ad-vaina	stranger
Inlitora	in-le-tora	on the coast
Opulentus	op-oo-lent-us	wealthy
Urbe Mortuos	ur-bey mor-too-oes	City of the Dead

Words	Pronunciation	Meaning
mea culpa	may-a cool-pa	my fault
Clepta Saccularius	klep-ta sack-oo-lar-ee-us	thief and cheat
Preceptum	pre-sep-tum	Sheriff
Trica	tree-ka	trouble
Dolor	do-lore	pain
ita fiat esto	eeta fee-it es-toe	so be it
Eremus	ae-ree-mus	desert
Libertus	lee-burt-us	freedom
Iggy (Ignavia)	eeg-nav-eea	sloth
Ira (Iracundia)	era-kon-dea	anger
Novellus	noe-vel-lus	youngest
prope mortem	proe-pay mor-tem	near dead
Regionem Cancellarii	ray-jo-nem kan-sel-laree	Regional Chancellor
justitia et pax	jus-teet-shia et paucks	Justice of the Peace
Jack Ominium Artium	jack omee-nium ar-toom	Jack of All Trades
mendacium	men-da-coom	lies
Amabilia	ama-bilia	lovely
Nugae	new-guy	idle talk, gossip
gestor	jes-ter	gossiper
forma libertas	for-ma lee-ber-tus	freeman papers
Insula Mortem	in-su-la mor-tam	Island of Death
Dentibus Igni Timens	den-tee-buss ee-nee tee-mans	of fire and teeth fearful
Calicem Bonitatem	ku-lech-um bon-ee-tat-um	The Cup of Goodness
Basil (Basileus)	baa-sul	King
Colonus	ko-lon-us	farmer
Germanus	jer-man-us	brother